DOCTOR DOLITTLE
IN THE MOON

THE YEARLING DOCTOR DOLITTLE BOOKS

YEARLING BOOKS/YOUNG YEARLINGS/YEARLING CLASSICS are designed especially to entertain and enlighten young people. Charles F. Reasoner, Professor Emeritus of Children's Literature and Reading, New York University, is consultant to this series.

For a complete listing of all Yearling titles,
write to Dell Readers Service,
P.O. Box 1045, South Holland, Illinois 60473.

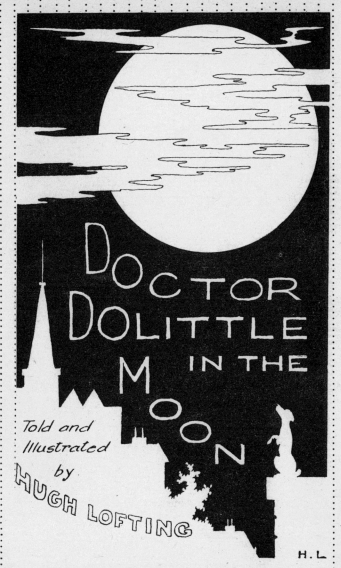

DOCTOR DOLITTLE IN THE MOON

Told and Illustrated by HUGH LOFTING

H.L

THE CENTENARY EDITION
A YEARLING BOOK

I would like to acknowledge the following editors whose faith in the literary value of these children's classics was invaluable in the publication of the new editions: Janet Chenery, consulting editor; Olga Fricker, Hugh Lofting's sister-in-law, who worked closely with the author and edited the last four original books; Lori Mack, associate editor at Dell; and Lois Myller, whose special love for Doctor Dolittle helped make this project possible.

CHRISTOPHER LOFTING

· Contents ·

· Illustrations ·

DOCTOR DOLITTLE
IN THE MOON

· The First Chapter ·
WE LAND UPON A NEW WORLD

In writing the story of our adventures in the moon I, Thomas Stubbins, secretary to John Dolittle, M.D. (and son of Jacob Stubbins, the cobbler of Puddleby-on-the-Marsh), find myself greatly puzzled. It is not an easy task, remembering day by day and hour by hour those crowded and exciting weeks. It is true I made many notes for the Doctor, books full of them. But that information was nearly all of a highly scientific kind. And I feel that I should tell the story here not for the scientist so much as for the general reader. And it is in that I am perplexed.

For the story could be told in many ways. People are so different in what they want to know about a voyage. I had thought at one time that Jip could help me; and after reading him some chapters as I had first set them down, I asked for his opinion. I discovered he was mostly interested in whether we had seen any rats in the moon. I found I could not tell him. I didn't remember seeing any, and yet I am sure there must have been some—or some sort of creature like a rat.

Then I asked Gub-Gub. And what he was chiefly concerned to hear was the kind of vegetables we had fed on. (Dab-Dab snorted at me for my pains and said I should have known better than to ask him.) I tried my mother. She wanted to know how we had managed when our underwear wore out—and a whole lot of other matters about our living conditions, hardly any of which I could answer. Next I went to Matthew Mugg. And the things he wanted to learn were worse than either my mother's or Jip's: Were there any shops in the moon? What were the dogs and cats like? The good cat's-meat man seemed to have imagined it a place not very different from Puddleby or the East End of London.

I couldn't seem to tell people any of the things they were most anxious to know. It reminded me of the first time I had come to the Doctor's house, hoping to be hired as his assistant, and dear old Polynesia the parrot had questioned me. "Are you a good noticer?" she had asked. I had always thought I was—pretty good, anyhow. But now I felt I had been a very poor noticer.

The trouble was of course *attention*. Human attention is like butter: you can only spread it so thin and no thinner. If you try to spread it over too many things at once, you just don't remember them. And certainly during all our waking hours upon the moon there was so much for our ears and eyes and minds to take in, it is a wonder, I often think, that any clear memories at all remain.

The one who could have been of most help to me in writing my impressions of the moon was Jamaro Bumblelily, the giant moth who carried us there. But as he was nowhere near me when I set to work upon this book, I decided I had better not consider the particular wishes of Jip, Gub-Gub, my mother, Matthew, or anyone else, but set the story down in my own way. Clearly, the tale must be in any case an imperfect, incomplete one. And the only thing to do is to go forward with it, step by step, to the best of my recollection, from where the great insect hovered, with our beating hearts pressed close against his broad back, over the near and glowing landscape of the moon.

Anyone could tell that the moth knew every detail of the country we were landing in. Planing, circling, and diving, he brought his wide-winged body very deliberately down toward a little valley fenced in with hills. The bottom of this, I saw as we drew nearer, was level, sandy, and dry.

The hills struck one at once as unusual. In fact, all the mountains as well (for much greater heights could presently be seen towering away in the dim greenish light behind the nearer, lower ranges) had one peculiarity. The tops seemed to be cut off and cuplike. The Doctor afterward explained to me that they were extinct volcanoes. Nearly all these peaks had once belched fire and molten lava but were now cold and dead. Some had been fretted and worn by winds and weather and time into quite curious shapes, and yet others had been filled up or half buried by drifting sand so that they had nearly lost the appearance of volcanoes. I was reminded of the Whispering Rocks that we had seen on Spidermonkey Island. And though this scene was different in many things, no one who had ever looked upon a volcanic landscape before could have mistaken it for anything else.

The little valley, long and narrow, that we were apparently making for did not show many signs of life, vegetable or animal. But we were not disturbed by that. At least the Doctor wasn't. He had seen a tree and he was satisfied that before long he would find water, vegetation, and creatures.

At last when the moth had dropped within twenty feet of the ground, he spread his wings motionless and like a great kite gently touched the sand, in hops at first, then ran a little, braced himself, and came to a standstill.

We had landed on the moon!

By this time we had had a chance to get a little more used to the new air. But before we made any attempt to "go ashore," the Doctor thought it best to ask our gallant steed to stay where he was a while, so that we could still further accustom ourselves to the new atmosphere and conditions.

This request was willingly granted. Indeed the poor insect himself, I imagine, was glad enough to rest a while. From somewhere in his packages John Dolittle produced an emergency ration of chocolate that he had been saving up. All four of us munched in silence, too hungry and too awed by our new surroundings to say a word.

The light changed unceasingly. It reminded me of the Northern Lights, the Aurora Borealis. You would gaze at the mountains above you, then turn away a moment, and on looking back find everything that had been pink was now green, the shadows that had been violet were rose.

Breathing was still kind of difficult. We were compelled for the moment to keep the moon bells handy. These were the great orange-colored flowers that the moth had brought down for us. It was their perfume (or gas) that had enabled us to cross the airless belt that lay between the moon and the earth. A fit of coughing was always liable to come on if one left them too long. But already we felt that we could, in time, get used to this new air and soon do without the bells altogether.

The gravity, too, was very confusing. It required hardly any effort to rise from a sitting position to a standing one. Walking was no effort at all—for the muscles—but for the lungs it was another question. The most extraordinary sensation was jumping. The least little spring from the ankles sent you flying into the air in the most fantastic fashion. If it had not been for this problem of breathing properly (which the Doctor seemed to feel we should approach with great caution, on account of its possible effect on the heart), we would all have given ourselves up to this most lighthearted feeling that took possession of us. I remember, myself, singing songs and I was most anxious to get down off the moth's back and go bounding

"Zip! The spring was made"

away across the hills and valleys to explore this new world.

But I realize now that John Dolittle was very wise in making us wait. He issued orders (in the low whispers that we found necessary in this new clear air) to each and all of us that for the present the flowers were *not* to be left behind for a single moment.

They were cumbersome things to carry, but we obeyed orders. No ladder was needed now to descend by. The gentlest jump sent one flying off the insect's back to the ground, where you landed from a twenty-five-foot drop with ease and comfort.

Zip! The spring was made. And we were wading in the sands of a new world.

· The Second Chapter ·
THE LAND OF COLORS
AND PERFUMES

We were after all a very odd party that made the first landing on a new world. But in a great many ways it was a peculiarly good combination. First of all, Polynesia was the kind of bird that one always supposed would exist under any conditions, drought, floods, fire, or frost. I've no doubt that I exaggerated Polynesia's adaptability and endurance. But even to this day I can never imagine any circumstances in which that remarkable bird would perish. If she could get a pinch of seed (of almost any kind) and a sip of water two or three times a week, she would not only carry on quite cheerfully but would scarcely even remark upon the strange nature or scantiness of the rations.

Then Chee-Chee: He was not so easily provided for in the matter of food. But he always seemed to be able to provide for himself anything that was lacking. I have never known a better forager than Chee-Chee. When everyone was hungry he could go off into an entirely new forest and just by smelling the wild

"By smelling he could tell if they were safe to eat"

fruits and nuts he could tell if they were safe to eat.
How he did this, even John Dolittle could never find
out. Indeed, Chee-Chee himself didn't know.

Then myself: I had no scientific qualifications, but I
had learned how to be a good secretary on natural-
history expeditions and I knew a good deal about the
Doctor's ways.

Finally there was the Doctor. No naturalist has
ever gone afield to grasp at the secrets of a new land
with the qualities John Dolittle possessed. He never

claimed to know anything, beforehand, for certain. He came to new problems with a childlike innocence that made it easy for himself to learn and the others to teach.

Yes, it was a strange party we made up. Most scientists would have laughed at us, no doubt. Yet we had many things to recommend us that no expedition ever carried before.

As usual, the Doctor wasted no time in preliminaries. Most other explorers would have begun by planting a flag and singing national anthems. Not so with John Dolittle. As soon as he was sure that we were all ready he gave the order to march. And without a word, Chee-Chee and I (with Polynesia, who perched herself on my shoulder) fell in behind him and started off.

I have never known a time when it was harder to shake loose the feeling of living in a dream as those first few hours we spent on the moon. The knowledge that we were treading a new world never before visited by Man, added to this extraordinary feeling, caused by the gravity, of lightness, of walking on air, made you want every minute to have someone tell you that you were actually awake and in your right senses. For this reason I kept constantly speaking to the Doctor or Chee-Chee or Polynesia—even when I had nothing particular to say. But the uncanny booming of my own voice every time I opened my lips and spoke above the faintest whisper merely added to the dreamlike effect of the whole experience.

However, little by little, we grew accustomed to it.

And certainly there was no lack of new sights and impressions to occupy our minds. Those strange and ever-changing colors in the landscape were most bewildering, throwing out your course and sense of direction entirely. The Doctor had brought a small pocket compass with him. But on consulting it, we saw that it was even more confused than we were. The needle did nothing but whirl around in the craziest fashion, and no amount of steadying would persuade it to stay still.

Giving that up, the Doctor determined to rely on his moon maps and his own eyesight and bump of locality. He was heading toward where he had seen that tree—which was at the end of one of the ranges. But all the ranges in this section seemed very much alike. The maps did not help us in this respect in the least. To our rear we could see certain peaks that we thought we could identify on the charts. But ahead, nothing fitted in at all. This made us feel surer than ever that we were moving toward the moon's other side, which earthly eyes had never seen.

"It is likely enough, Stubbins," said the Doctor as we strode lightly forward over loose sand, which would ordinarily have been very heavy going, "that it is *only* on the other side that water exists. Which may partly be the reason why astronomers never believed there was any here at all."

For my part I was so on the lookout for extraordinary sights that it did not occur to me, till the Doctor spoke of it, that the temperature was extremely mild and agreeable. One of the things that John Dolittle

"The Doctor had brought a compass"

had feared was that we should find a heat that was
unbearable or a cold that was worse than arctic. But
except for the difficulty of the strange new quality of
the air, no human could have asked for a nicer climate. A gentle steady wind was blowing and the temperature seemed to remain almost constantly the
same.

We looked about everywhere for tracks. As yet we
knew very little of what animal life to expect. But the
loose sand told nothing, not even to Chee-Chee, who

"Jumping was extraordinarily easy"

was a pretty experienced hand at picking up tracks of the most unusual kind.

Of odors and scents there were plenty—most of them very delightful flower perfumes, which the wind brought to us from the other side of the mountain ranges ahead. Occasionally a very disagreeable one would come, mixed up with the pleasant scents. But none of them, except that of the moon bells the moth had brought with us, could we recognize.

On and on we went for miles, crossing ridge after

ridge and still no glimpse did we get of the Doctor's tree. Of course, crossing the ranges was not nearly as hard traveling as it would have been on earth. Jumping and bounding both upward and downward was extraordinarily easy. Still, we had brought a good deal of baggage with us and all of us were pretty heavy-laden; and after two and a half hours of travel we began to feel a little discouraged. Polynesia then volunteered to fly ahead and reconnoiter, but this the Doctor was loath to have her do. For some reason, he wanted us all to stick together for the present.

However, after another half hour of going he consented to let her fly straight up, so long as she remained in sight, to see if she could spy out the tree's position from a greater height.

· The Third Chapter ·
THIRST!

So we rested on our bundles a spell while Polynesia gave an imitation of a soaring vulture and climbed and climbed straight above our heads. At about a thousand feet she paused and circled. Then slowly came down again. The Doctor, watching her, grew impatient at her speed. I could not quite make out why he was so unwilling to have her away from his side, but I asked no questions.

Yes, she had seen the tree, she told us, but it still seemed a long way off. The Doctor wanted to know why she had taken so long in coming down and she said she had been making sure of her bearings so that she would be able to act as guide. Indeed, with the usual accuracy of birds, she had a very clear idea of the direction we should take. And we set off again, feeling more at ease and confident.

The truth of it was, of course, that seen from a great height, as the tree had first appeared to us, the distance had seemed much less than it actually was.

Two more things helped to mislead us. One, that the moon air, as we now discovered, made everything look nearer than it actually was, in spite of the soft, dim light. And the other was that we had supposed the tree to be one of ordinary earthly size and, unconscious, had made a guess at its distance in keeping with a fair-sized oak or elm. Whereas when we did actually reach it, we found it to be unimaginably huge.

I shall never forget that tree. It was our first experience of moon life, *in* the moon. Darkness was coming on when we finally halted beneath it. When I say *darkness* I mean that strange kind of twilight that was the nearest thing to night we ever saw in the moon. The tree's height, I should say, would be at least three hundred feet and the width of it across the trunk a good forty or fifty. Its appearance in general was most uncanny. The whole design of it was different from any tree I have ever seen. Yet there was no mistaking it for anything else. It seemed—*alive*. Poor Chee-Chee was so scared of it his hair just stood up on the nape of his neck, and it was a long time before the Doctor and I persuaded him to help us pitch camp beneath its boughs.

Indeed, we were a very subdued party that prepared to spend its first night on the moon. No one knew just what it was that oppressed us, but we were all conscious of a definite feeling of disturbance. The wind still blew—in that gentle, steady way that the moon winds always blew. The light was clear enough to see outlines by, although most of the night the

"It was different from any tree I have ever seen"

earth was invisible and there was no reflection whatever.

I remember how the Doctor, while we were unpacking and laying out the rest of our chocolate ration for supper, kept glancing uneasily up at those strange limbs of the tree overhead.

Of course, it was the wind that was moving them—no doubt of that at all. Yet the wind was so deadly regular and even. And the movement of the boughs

HUGH LOFTING

"The Doctor kept glancing up uneasily"

wasn't regular at all. That was the weird part of it. It almost seemed as though the tree were doing some moving on its own, like an animal chained by its feet in the ground. And still you could never be sure—because, after all, the wind *was* blowing all the time.

And besides, it moaned. Well, we knew trees moaned in the wind at home. But this one did it differently—it didn't seem in keeping with that regular, even wind that we felt upon our faces.

I could see that even the worldly-wise, practical
Polynesia was perplexed and upset. And it took a
great deal to disturb her. Yet a bird's senses toward
trees and winds are much keener than a man's. I kept
hoping she would venture into the branches of the
tree, but she didn't. And as for Chee-Chee, also a natural denizen of the forest, no power on earth, I felt
sure, would persuade him to investigate the mysteries of this strange specimen of a vegetable kingdom
we were as yet only distantly acquainted with.

After supper was dispatched, the Doctor kept me
busy for some hours taking down notes. There was
much to be recorded of this first day in a new world.
The temperature, the direction and force of the wind,
the time of our arrival—as near as it could be guessed
—the air pressure (he had brought along a small ba-
rometer among his instruments), and many other
things that, while they were dry stuff for the ordinary
mortal, were highly important for the scientist.

Often and often I have wished that I had one of
those memories that seem to be able to recall all impressions, no matter how small and unimportant. For
instance, I have often wanted to remember exactly
that first awakening on the moon. We had all been
weary enough with excitement and exercise, when
we went to bed, to sleep soundly. All I can remember
of my waking up is spending at least ten minutes
working out where I was. And I doubt if I could have
done it even then if I had not finally realized that
John Dolittle was awake ahead of me and already
pottering around among his instruments, taking
readings.

The immediate business now on hand was food. There was literally nothing for breakfast. The Doctor began to regret his hasty departure from the moth. Indeed it was only now, many, many hours after we had left him in our haste to find the tree and explore the new world, that we realized that we had not yet seen any signs of animal life. Still, it seemed a long way to go back and consult him, and it was by no means certain that he would still be there.

Just the same, we needed to find food. Hastily we bundled together what things we had unpacked for the night's camping. Which way to go? Clearly, if we had here reached one tree, there must be some direction in which others lay, where we could find that water that the Doctor was so sure must exist. But we could scan the horizon with staring eyes or telescope as much as we wished, and not another leaf of a tree could we see.

This time, without waiting to be ordered, Polynesia soared into the air to do a little scouting.

"Well," she said on her return, "I don't see any actual trees at all. The beastly landscape is more like the Sahara Desert than any scenery I've ever run into. But over there behind that higher range—the one with the curious hat-shaped peak in the middle—you see the one I mean?"

"Yes," said the Doctor. "I see. Go on."

"Well, behind that there is a dark horizon different from any other quarter. I won't swear it is trees. But myself, I feel convinced that there is something else there besides sand. We had better get moving. It is no short walk."

"Polynesia soared into the air"

Indeed it *was* no short walk. It came to be a forced march or race between us and starvation. On starting out we had not foreseen anything of the kind. Going off without breakfast was nothing, after all. Each one of us had done that before many a time. But as hour after hour went by and still the landscape remained a desert of rolling sand dunes, hills, and dead, dry volcanoes, our spirits fell lower and lower.

This was one of the times when I think I saw John Dolittle really at his best. I know, although I had not

"I remember Chee-Chee trickling something cool
between my lips"

questioned him, that he had already been beset with
anxiety over several matters on the first steps of our
march. Later he spoke of them to me: not at the time.
And as conditions grew worse, as hunger gnawed at
our vitals and the most terrible thirst parched our
tongues—as strength and vitality began to give way
and mere walking became the most terrible hardship,
the Doctor grew cheerier and cheerier. He didn't
crack dry jokes in an irritating way, either. But by

some strange means he managed to keep the whole party in a good mood. If he told a funny story it was always at the right time and set us all laughing at our troubles. In talking to him afterward about this I learned that he had, when a young man, been employed on more than one exploration trip to keep the expedition in good humor. It was, he said, the only way he could persuade the chief to take him, since at that time he had no scientific training to recommend him.

Anyway, I sincerely doubt whether our party would have held out if it had not been for his sympathetic and cheering company. The agonies of thirst were something new to me. Every step I thought must be my last.

Finally, at what seemed to be the end of our second day, I vaguely heard Polynesia saying something about "Forests ahead!" I imagine I must have been half delirious by then. I still staggered along, blindly following the others. I know we *did* reach water because, before I fell and dozed away into a sort of half faint, I remember Chee-Chee trickling something marvelously cool between my lips out of a cup made from a folded leaf.

· The Fourth Chapter ·

CHEE-CHEE THE HERO

When I awoke I felt very much ashamed of myself. What an explorer! The Doctor was moving around already—and, of course, Chee-Chee and Polynesia. John Dolittle came to my side as soon as he saw I was awake.

As though he knew the thoughts that were in my mind, he at once started to reprimand me for feeling ashamed of my performance. He pointed out that, after all, Chee-Chee and Polynesia were accustomed to traveling in hot, dry climates and that so, for that matter, was he himself.

"Taken all in all, Stubbins," said he, "your own performance has been extremely good. You made the trip the whole way and collapsed only when relief was in sight. No one could ask for more than that. I have known many experienced explorers who couldn't have done nearly as well. It was a hard lap— a devilish hard lap. You were magnificent. Sit up and have some breakfast. Thank goodness, we've reached food at last!"

Weak and frowsty, I sat up. Arranged immediately around me was a collection of what I later learned were fruits. The reliable Chee-Chee, scared though he might be of a moving tree or a whispering wind, had served the whole party with that wonderful sense of his for scenting out wild foodstuffs. Not one of the strange courses on the bill of fare had I or the Doctor seen before. But if Chee-Chee said they were safe we knew we need not fear.

Some of the fruits were as big as a large trunk; some as small as a walnut. But, starving as we were, we just dived in and ate and ate and ate. Water there was too, gathered in the shells of enormous nuts and odd vessels made from twisted leaves. Never has a breakfast tasted so marvelous as did that one of fruits that I could not name.

Chee-Chee! Poor little timid Chee-Chee, who conquered your own fears and volunteered to go ahead of us, alone, into the jungle to find food when our strength was giving out. To the world you were just an organ-grinder's monkey. But to us, whom you saved from starvation when terror beset you at every step, you will forever be ranked high in the list of the great heroes of all time. Thank goodness we had you with us! Our bones might today be moldering in the sands of the moon if it had not been for your untaught science, your jungle skill—and, above all, your courage that overcame your fear!

Well, to return: As I ate these strange fruits and

HUGH LOFTING

"Some of the fruits were as big as a trunk"

sipped the water that brought life back, I gazed upward and saw before me a sort of ridge. On its level
top a vegetation, a kind of tangled forest, flourished;
and trailing down from this ridge were little outposts
of the vegetable kingdom, groups of bushes and single trees that scattered and dribbled away in several
directions from the main mass. Why and how that
lone tree survived so far away we could never satis-
factorily explain. The nearest John Dolittle could
come to it was that some underground spring sup-

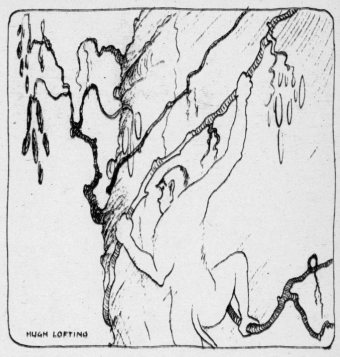

" 'I climbed a tree' "

plied it with enough water or moisture to carry on. Yet there can be no doubt that to have reached such enormous proportions it must have been there hundreds—perhaps thousands—of years. Anyway, it is a good thing for us it *was* there. If it had not been, as a pointer toward this habitable quarter of the moon—it is most likely our whole expedition would have perished.

When the Doctor and I had finished our mysterious breakfast, we started to question Chee-Chee about the

"We approached the bluff on whose brow
the vegetation flourished"

forest from which he had produced the food we had
eaten.

"I don't know how I did it," said Chee-Chee when
we asked him, "I just shut my eyes most of the time—
terribly afraid. I passed trees, plants, creepers, roots.
I smelled . . . Goodness! I, too, was hungry, remember. I smelled hard as I could. And soon of course I
spotted food, fruits. I climbed a tree—half the time
with my eyes shut. Then I see some monster, golly!

What a jungle—different from any monkey ever see before! Woolly, woolly! Ooh, ooh! All the same, nuts smell good. Catch a few. Chase down the tree. Run some more. Smell again. Good! Up another tree. Different fruit—good just the same. Catch a few. Down again. Run home. On the way smell good root. Same as ginger—only better. Dig a little. Keep eyes shut—don't want to see monster. Catch a piece of root. Run all the way home. Here I am. Finish!"

Well, dear old Chee-Chee's story was descriptive of his own heroic adventures, but it did not give us much idea of the moon forest that we were to explore. Nevertheless, rested and fit, we now felt much more inclined to look into things ourselves.

Leaving what luggage we had brought with us from our original landing point, we proceeded toward the line of trees at the summit of the bluff, about four miles ahead of us. We now felt that we could find our way back without much difficulty to the two last camps we had established.

The going was about the same, loose sand—only that as we approached the bluff we found the sand firmer to the tread.

On the way up the last lap toward the vegetation line we were out of view of the top itself. Often the going was steep. All the way, I had the feeling that we were about to make new and great discoveries—that for the first time we were to learn something important about the true nature of the mysterious moon.

· The Fifth Chapter ·
ON THE PLATEAU

Indeed, our first close acquaintance with the forests of the moon was made in quite a dramatic manner. Suddenly, as our heads topped the bluff, we saw a wall of jungle some mile or so ahead of us. It would take a very long time to describe those trees in detail. It wasn't that there were so many kinds, but each one was so utterly different from any tree we had seen on the earth. And yet, curiously enough, they did remind you of vegetable forms you had seen, but not of trees.

For instance, there was one whole section, several square miles in extent apparently, that looked exactly like ferns. Another reminded me of a certain flowering plant (I can't recall the name of it) that grows a vast number of small blossoms on a flat surface at the top. The stems are a curious whitish green. This moon tree was *exactly* the same, only nearly a thousand times as big. The denseness of the foliage (or flowering) at the top was so compact and solid that

"The umbrella tree"

we later found no rain could penetrate it. And for this
reason the Doctor and I gave it the name of the *umbrella tree*. But not one single tree was there that was
the same as any tree we had seen before. And there
were many, many more curious growths that dimly
reminded you of something, though you could not
always say exactly what.

One odd thing that disturbed us quite a little was a
strange sound. Noises of any kind, no matter how
faint, we already knew could travel long distances on

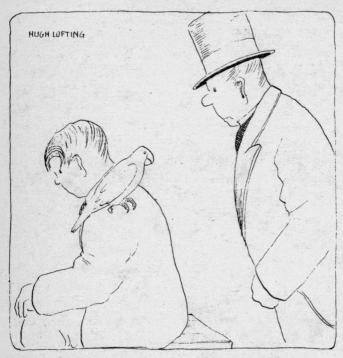

HUGH LOFTING

" 'Yes,' said she, 'I was awake several times' "

the moon. As soon as we had gained the plateau on top of the bluff we heard it. It was a musical sound. And yet not the sound of a single instrument. It seemed almost as though there was a small orchestra somewhere playing very, very softly. We were, by this time, becoming accustomed to strange things. But I must confess that this distant hidden music upset me quite a little and so, I know, it did the Doctor.

At the top of the bluff we rested to get our wind before we covered the last mile up to the jungle itself.

It was curious how clearly marked and separated were those sections of the moon's landscape. And yet doubtless the smaller scale of all the geographical features of this world, so much less in bulk than our own, could partly account for that. In front of us a plateau stretched out, composed of hard sand, level and smooth as a lake, bounded in front by the jungle and to the rear of us by the cliff we had just scaled. I wondered, as I looked across at the forest, what scenery began on the other side of the woods and if it broke off in as sharp a change as it did here.

As the most important thing to attend to first was the establishment of a water supply, Chee-Chee was asked to act as guide. The monkey set out ahead of us to follow his own tracks that he had made last night. This he had little difficulty in doing across the open plateau. But when we reached the edge of the forest it was not so easy. Much of his traveling here had been done by swinging through the trees. He always felt safer so, he said, while explaining to us how he had been guided to the water by the sense of smell.

Again I realized how lucky we had been to have him with us. No one but a monkey could have found his way through that dense, dimly lit forest to water. He asked us to stay behind a moment on the edge of the woods while he went forward to make sure that he could retrace his steps. We sat down again and waited.

"Did you wake up at all during the night, Stubbins?" the Doctor asked after a little.

"No," I said. "I was far too tired. Why?"

"Did you, Polynesia?" he asked, ignoring my question.

"Yes," said she. "I was awake several times."

"Did you hear or see anything—er—unusual?"

"Yes," said she. "I can't be absolutely certain, but I sort of felt there was something moving around the camp keeping a watch on us."

"Humph!" muttered the Doctor. "So did I."

Then he relapsed into silence.

Another rather strange thing that struck me as I gazed over the landscape, while we waited for Chee-Chee to return, was the appearance of the horizon. The moon's width being so much smaller than the earth's, the distance one could see was a great deal shorter. This did not apply so much where the land was hilly or mountainous, but on the level, or the nearly level, it made a very striking difference. The *roundness* of this world was much more easily felt and understood than was that of the world we had left. On this plateau, for example, you could only see seven or eight miles, it seemed, over the level before the curve cut off your vision. And it gave quite a new character even to the hills, where peaks showed behind other ranges, dropping downward in a way that misled you entirely as to their actual height.

Finally Chee-Chee came back to us and said he had successfully retraced his steps to the water he had found the night before. He was now prepared to lead us to it. He looked kind of scared and ill at ease. The Doctor asked him the reason for this, but he didn't seem able to give any.

"Everything's all right, Doctor," said he, "—at least

"The *roundness* of this world was much more easily felt"

I suppose it is. It was partly that—oh, I don't know—I
can't quite make out what it is they have asked you
here for. I haven't actually laid eyes on any animal

HUGH LOFTING

" 'You bet they were not!' grunted Polynesia"

life since we left the moth who brought us. Yet I feel certain that there's lots of it here. It doesn't appear to want to be seen. That's what puzzles me. On the earth the animals were never slow in coming forward when they were in need of your services."

"You bet they were not!" grunted Polynesia. "No one who ever saw them clamoring around the surgery door could doubt that."

"Humph!" the Doctor muttered. "I've noticed it myself already. I don't understand it quite, either. It al-

most looks as though there were something about
our arrival that they didn't like . . . I wonder . . .
Well, anyway, I wish the animal life here would get in
touch with us and let us know what it is all about.
This state of things is, to say the least—er—upset-
ting."

· The Sixth Chapter ·

THE MOON LAKE

And so we went forward with Chee-Chee as guide to find the water. Our actual entrance into that jungle was quite an experience and very different from merely a distant view of it. The light outside was not bright; inside the woods it was dimmer still. My only other experience of jungle life had been on Spidermonkey Island. This was something like the Spidermonkey forest and yet it was strikingly different.

From the appearance and size of that first tree we had reached, the Doctor had guessed its age to be very, very great. Here the vegetable life in general seemed to bear out that idea beyond all question. The enormous trees with their gigantic trunks looked as though they had been there since the beginning of time. And there was surprisingly little decay—a few shed limbs and leaves. That was all. In unkept earthly forests one saw dead trees everywhere, fallen to the ground or caught halfway in the crotches of other

trees, withered and dry. Not so here. Every tree
looked as though it had stood so and grown in peace
for centuries.

At length after a good deal of arduous travel—the
going for the most part was made slow by the heavi-
est kind of undergrowth, with vines and creepers as
thick as your leg—we came to a sort of open place in
which lay a broad, calm lake with a pleasant water-
fall at one end. The woods that surrounded it were
most peculiar. They looked like enormous asparagus.
For many, many square miles their tremendous
masts rose close together in ranks. No creepers or
vines had here been given a chance to flourish. The
enormous stalks had taken up all the room and the
nourishment of the crowded earth. The tapering tops,
hundreds of feet above our heads, looked good
enough to eat. Yet I've no doubt that, if we had ever
gotten up to them, they would have been found as
hard as oaks.

The Doctor walked down to the clean sandy shore
of the lake and tried the water. Chee-Chee and I did
the same. It was pure and clear and quenching to the
thirst. The lake must have been at least five miles
wide in the center.

"I would like," said John Dolittle, "to explore this
by boat. Do you suppose, Chee-Chee, that we could
find the makings of a canoe or a raft anywhere?"

"I should think so," said the monkey. "Wait a minute and I will take a look around and see."

So, with Chee-Chee in the lead, we proceeded along
the shore in search of materials for a boat. On account of that scarcity of dead or dried wood that we

had already noticed, our search did not at first appear a very promising one. Nearly all the standing trees were pretty heavy and full of sap. For our work of boat-building a light hatchet on the Doctor's belt was the best tool we had. It looked sadly small compared with the great timber that reared up from the shores of the lake.

But after we had gone along about a mile I noticed Chee-Chee up ahead stop and peer into the jungle. Then, after he had motioned to us with his hand to hurry, he disappeared into the edge of the forest. On coming up with him we found him stripping the creepers and moss off some contrivance that lay just within the woods, not more than a hundred yards from the water's edge.

We all fell to, helping him, without any idea of what it might be we were uncovering. There seemed almost no end to it. It was a long object, immeasurably long. To me it looked like a dead tree—the first dead, lying tree we had seen.

"What do you think it is, Chee-Chee?" asked the Doctor.

"It's a boat," said the monkey in a firm and matter-of-fact voice. "No doubt of it at all in my mind. It's a dugout canoe. They used to use them in Africa."

"But, Chee-Chee," cried John Dolittle, "look at the length! It's a full-sized asparagus tree. We've uncovered a hundred feet of it already and still there's more to come."

"I can't help that," said Chee-Chee. "It's a dugout canoe just the same. Crawl down with me here underneath it, Doctor, and I'll show you the marks of tools and fire. It has been turned upside down."

With the monkey guiding him, the Doctor scrabbled down below the queer object; and when he came forth there was a puzzled look on his face.

"Well, they *might* be the marks of tools, Chee-Chee," he was saying. "But then again they might not. The traces of fire are more clear. But that could be accidental. If the tree burned down it could very easily—"

"The natives in my part of Africa," Chee-Chee interrupted, "always used fire to eat out the insides of their dug-out canoes. They built little fires all along the tree to hollow out the trunk so that they could sit in it. The tools they used were very simple, just stone scoops to chop out the charred wood with. I am sure this is a canoe, Doctor. But it hasn't been used in a long time. See how the bow has been shaped up into a point."

"I know," said the Doctor. "But the asparagus tree has a natural point at one end, anyhow."

"And, Chee-Chee," put in Polynesia, "who in the name of goodness could ever handle such a craft? Why, look, the thing is as long as a battleship!"

Then followed a half-hour's discussion, between the Doctor and Polynesia on the one side and Chee-Chee on the other, as to whether the find we had made was or was not a canoe. For me, I had no opinion. To my eyes the object looked like an immensely long log, hollowed somewhat on the one side, but whether by accident or design I could not tell.

In any case, it was certainly too heavy and

cumbersome for us to use. And presently I edged into the argument with the suggestion that we go on farther and find materials for a raft or boat we *could* handle.

The Doctor seemed rather glad of this excuse to end a fruitless controversy, and soon we moved on in search of something that would enable us to explore the waters of the lake. A march of a mile farther along the shore brought us to woods that were not so heavy. Here the immense asparagus forests gave way to a growth of smaller girth, and the Doctor's hatchet soon felled enough poles for us to make a raft from. We laced them together with thongs of bark and found them sufficiently buoyant when launched to carry us and our small supply of baggage with ease. Where the water was shallow we used a long pole to punt with; and when we wished to explore greater depths we employed sweeps, or oars, which we fashioned roughly with the hatchet.

From the first moment we were afloat the Doctor kept me busy taking notes for him. In the equipment he had brought with him there was a fine-meshed landing net, and with it he searched along the shores for signs of life in this moon lake, the first of its kind we had met with.

"It is very important, Stubbins," said he, "to find out what fish we have here. In evolution the fish life is a very important matter."

"What is *evolution?*" asked Chee-Chee.

I started out to explain it to him but was soon called upon by the Doctor to make more notes—for which I was not sorry, as the task turned out to be a

HUGH LOFTING

"We used a long pole to punt with"

long and heavy one. Polynesia, however, took it up where I left off and made short work of it.

"Evolution, Chee-Chee," said she, "is the story of how Tommy got rid of the tail you are carrying— because he didn't need it anymore—and the story of how you grew it and kept it because you *did* need it. *Evolution! Poof!* Professors' talk. A long word for a simple matter."

It turned out that our examination of the lake was neither exciting nor profitable. We brought up all sorts of water flies, many larvae of perfectly tremendous size, but we found as yet no fishes. The plant life —water plant I mean—was abundant.

"I think," said the Doctor, after we had poled ourselves around the lake for several hours, "that there can be no doubt now that the vegetable kingdom here is much more important than the animal kingdom. And what there is of the animal kingdom seems to be mostly insect. However, we will camp on the shore of this pleasant lake and perhaps we shall see more later."

So we brought our raft to anchor at about the place from which we had started out and pitched camp on a stretch of clean yellow sand.

I shall never forget that night. It was uncanny. None of us slept well. All through the hours of darkness we heard things moving around us. Enormous things. Yet never did we see them or find out what they were. The four of us were nevertheless certain that all night we were being watched. Even Polynesia was disturbed. There seemed no doubt that there was plenty of animal life in the moon, but that it did not as yet want to show itself to us. The newness of our surroundings alone was disturbing enough, without this very uncomfortable feeling that something had made the moon folks distrustful of us.

· The Seventh Chapter ·

TRACKS OF A GIANT

Another thing that added to our sleeplessness that night was the continuance of the mysterious music. But then, so many strange things contributed to our general mystification and vague feeling of anxiety that it is hard to remember and distinguish them all.

The next morning after breakfasting on what remained of our fruits, we packed up and started off for further exploration. While the last of the packing had been in progress Chee-Chee and Polynesia had gone ahead to do a little advanced scouting for us. They formed an admirable team for such work. Polynesia would fly above the forest and get long-distance impressions from the air of what lay ahead while Chee-Chee would examine the more lowly levels of the route to be followed, from the trees and the ground.

The Doctor and I were just helping one another on with our packs when Chee-Chee came rushing back

" 'What do you think, Doctor?' he stammered"

to us in great excitement. His teeth were chattering so he could hardly speak.

"What do you think, Doctor!" he stammered. "We've found tracks back there. Tracks of a man! But so enormous, you've no idea! Come quick and I'll show you."

The Doctor looked up sharply at the scared and excited monkey, pausing a moment as though about to question him. Then he seemed to change his mind and turned once more to the business of taking up the baggage. With loads hoisted we gave a last glance around the camping ground to see if anything had been forgotten or left.

Our route did not lie directly across the lake, which mostly sprawled away to the right of our line of march. But we had to make our way partly around the lower end of it. Wondering what new chapter lay ahead of us, we fell in behind Chee-Chee and in silence started off along the shore.

After about half an hour's march we came to the mouth of a river that ran into the upper end of the lake. Along the margin of this we followed Chee-Chee for what seemed like another mile or so. Soon the shores of the stream widened out and the woods fell back quite a distance from the water's edge. The nature of the ground was still clean, firm sand. Presently we saw Polynesia's tiny figure ahead, waiting for us.

When we drew up with her we saw that she was standing by an enormous footprint. There was no doubt about its being a man's, clear in every detail. It was the most gigantic thing I have ever seen, a barefoot track fully four yards in length. There wasn't only one, either. Down the shore the trail went on for a considerable distance, and the span that the prints lay apart gave one some idea of the enormous stride of the giant who had left this trail behind him.

Questioning and alarmed, Chee-Chee and Polynesia gazed silently up at the Doctor for an explanation.

"Humph!" he muttered after a while. "So Man is here, too. My goodness, what a monster! Let us follow the trail."

HUGH LOFTING

"An enormous footprint"

Chee-Chee was undoubtedly scared of such a plan. It was clearly both his and Polynesia's idea that the farther we got away from the maker of those tracks the better. I could see terror and fright in the eyes of both of them. But neither made any objection; and in silence we plodded along, following in the path of this strange human who must, it would seem, be something out of a fairy tale.

But alas! It was not more than a mile farther on that the footprints turned into the woods, where, on

the mosses and leaves beneath the trees, no traces
had been left at all. Then we turned about and followed the river quite a distance to see if the creature
had come back out on the sands again. But never a
sign could we see. Chee-Chee spent a good deal of
time too, at the Doctor's request, trying to find his
path through the forest by any signs, such as broken
limbs or marks in the earth, that he might have left
behind. But not another trace could we find. Decid-
ing that he had merely come down to the stream to
get a drink, we gave up the pursuit and turned back
to the line of our original march.

Again I was thankful that I had company on that
expedition. It was certainly a most curious and extraordinary experience. None of us spoke very much,
but when we did it seemed that all of us had been
thinking the same things.

The woods grew more and more mysterious, and
more and more *alive,* as we went onward toward the
other side of the moon, the side that earthly Man had
never seen before. For one thing, the strange music
seemed to increase; and for another, there was more
movement in the limbs of the trees. Great branches
that looked like arms, bunches of small twigs that
could have been hands, swung and moved and
clawed the air in the most uncanny fashion. And always that steady wind went on blowing—even, regular, and smooth.

All of the forest was not gloomy, however. Much of
it was unbelievably beautiful. Acres of woods there
were that presented nothing but a gigantic sea of
many-colored blossoms, colors that seemed like

HUGH LOFTING

"There was more movement in the limbs of the trees"

something out of a dream, indescribable, yet clear in one's memory as a definite picture of something seen.

The Doctor, as we went forward, spoke very little. When he did, it was almost always on the same subject: "the absence of decay," as he put it.

"I am utterly puzzled, Stubbins," said he, in one of his longer outbursts when we were resting. "Why, there is hardly any leaf mold at all!"

"What difference would that make, Doctor?" I asked.

"Well, that's what the trees live on mostly, in our world," said he. "The forest growth, I mean—the soil that is formed by dying trees and rotting leaves—that is the nourishment that brings forth the seedlings that finally grow into new trees. But here! Well, of course there is *some* soil—and some shedding of leaves. But I've hardly seen a dead tree since I've been in these woods. One would almost think that there were some—er—balance. Some *arrangement* of —er—well, I can't explain it . . . It beats me entirely."

I did not at the time completely understand what he meant. And yet it did seem as though every one of these giant plants that rose about us led a life of peaceful growth, undisturbed by rot, by blight, or by disease.

Suddenly in our march we found ourselves at the end of the wooded section. Hills and mountains again spread before us. They were not the same as those we had first seen, however. These had vegetation, of a kind, on them. Low shrubs and heath plants clothed this rolling land with a dense growth—often very difficult to get through.

But still no sign of decay—little or no leaf mold. The Doctor now decided that perhaps part of the reason for this was the seasons—or rather the lack of seasons. He said that we would probably find that here there was no regular winter or summer. It was an entirely new problem, so far as the struggle for existence was concerned, such as we knew in our world.

· The Eighth Chapter ·
THE SINGING TREES

Into this new heath and hill country we traveled for miles. And presently we arrived upon a rather curious thing. It was a sort of basin high up and enclosed by hills or knolls. The strange part of it was that here there were not only more tracks of the giant man, just as we had seen lower down, but there were also unmistakable signs of *fire*. In an enormous hollow ashes lay among the sands. The Doctor was very interested in those ashes. He took some and added chemicals to them and tested them in many ways. He confessed himself at last entirely puzzled by their nature. But he said he nevertheless felt quite sure we had stumbled on the scene of the smoke-signaling we had seen from Puddleby. Curiously long ago, it seemed, that time when Too-Too the owl had insisted he saw smoke burst from the side of the moon. That was when the giant moth lay helpless in our garden. And yet—how long was it? Only a few days!

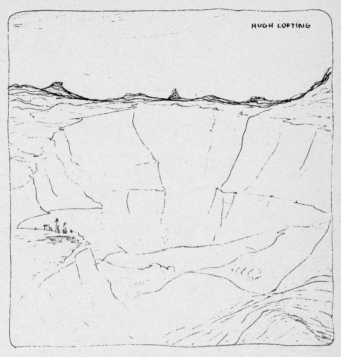

"It was a sort of basin"

"It was from here, Stubbins," said the Doctor, "that the signals we saw from the earth were given out, I feel certain. This place, as you see, is miles and miles across. But what was used to make an explosion as large as the one we saw from my house I have no idea."

"But it was smoke we saw," said I, "not a flash."

"That's just it," he said. "Some curious material must have been used that we have as yet no knowledge of. I thought that by testing the ashes I could discover what it was. But I can't. However, we may yet find out."

For two reasons the Doctor was anxious for the present not to get too far from the forest section. (We did not know then, you see, that there were other wooded areas besides this through which we had just come.) One reason was that we had to keep in touch with our food supply, which consisted of the fruits and vegetables of the jungle. The other was that John Dolittle was absorbed now in the study of this vegetable kingdom, which he felt sure had many surprises in store for the student naturalist.

After a while, we began to get over the feeling of uncanny creepiness, which at the beginning had made us so uncomfortable. We decided that our fears were mostly caused by the fact that these woods and plants were so different from our own. There was no unfriendliness in these forests after all, we assured ourselves—except that we *were* being watched. That we knew—and that we were beginning to get used to.

As soon as the Doctor had decided that we would set up our new headquarters on the edge of the forest, and we had our camp properly established, we began making excursions in all directions through the jungle. And from then on I was again kept very busy taking notes of the Doctor's experiments and studies.

One of the first discoveries we made in our study of the moon's vegetable kingdom was that there was practically no warfare going on between it and the animal kingdom. In the world we had left we had been accustomed to see the horses and other creatures eating up the grass in great quantities and many further examples of the struggle that continually goes on between the two. Here, on the other hand, the animals (or, more strictly speaking, the insects, for there seemed as yet hardly any traces of other animal species) and the vegetable life seemed, for the most part, to help one another rather than to fight and destroy. Indeed, we found the whole system of life on the moon a singularly peaceful business. I will speak of this again later on.

We spent three whole days in the investigation of the strange music we had heard. You will remember that the Doctor, with his skill on the flute, was naturally fond of music; and this curious thing we had met with interested him a great deal. After several expeditions we found patches of the jungle where we were able to see and hear the tree music working at its best.

There was no doubt about it at all: The trees were making the sounds and they were doing it *deliberately*. In the way that an Aeolian harp works when set in the wind at the right angle, the trees moved their branches to meet the wind so that certain notes would be given out. The evening that the Doctor made this discovery of what he called the *singing trees*, he told me to mark down in the diary of the expedition as a red-letter date. I shall never forget it. We had been following the sound for hours, the Doctor carrying a tuning fork in his hand, ringing it every once in a while to make sure of the notes we heard around us. Suddenly we came upon a little clearing about which great giants of the forest stood in a circle. It was for all the world like an orchestra. Spellbound, we stood and gazed up at them, as first one and then another would turn a branch to the steady, blowing wind and a note would boom out upon the night, clear and sweet. Then a group—three or four trees around the glade—would swing a limb and a chord would strike the air, and go murmuring through the jungle. Fantastic and crazy as it sounds, no one could have any doubt who heard and watched that these trees were actually making sounds that they *wanted to make*, with the aid of the wind.

Of course, as the Doctor remarked, unless the wind had always blown steadily and evenly such a thing would have been impossible. John Dolittle himself was most anxious to find out on what scale of music they were working. To me, I must confess, it sounded just mildly pleasant. There *was* a time: I could hear that. And some whole phrases were repeated once in a while, but not often. For the most part the melody was wild, sad, and strange. But even to my uneducated ear it was, beyond all question, a quite clear effort at orchestration; there were certainly treble voices and bass voices, and the combination was sweet and agreeable.

I was excited enough myself, but the Doctor was worked up to a pitch of interest such as I have seldom seen in him.

"Why, Stubbins," said he, "do you realize what this means? It's terrific. If these trees can sing—a choir understands one another and all that—*they must have a language*. They can talk! A language in the

"Spellbound, we gazed up at them"

vegetable kingdom! We must get after it. Who knows, I may yet learn it myself! Stubbins, this is a great day!"

And so, as usual on such occasions, the good man's enthusiasm just carried him away bodily. For days, often without food, often without sleep, he pursued this new study. And at his heels I trotted with my notebook always ready—though, to be sure, he put in far more work than I did because frequently when we got home he would go on wrestling for hours over

HUGH LOFTING

"For quite a long while he sat watching certain shrubs"

the notes or new apparatus he was building, by which he hoped to learn the language of the trees.

Even before we left the earth John Dolittle had mentioned the possibility of the moon bells having some means of communicating with one another. That they could move, within the limits of their fixed position, had been fully established. We had grown so used to it that we no longer thought anything of it. In fact, the Doctor had wondered if this might possibly be a means of conversation in itself—the movement of limbs and twigs and leaves, something like a flag signal-code. And for quite a long while he sat watching certain trees and shrubs to see if they used this method for talking between themselves.

· The Ninth Chapter ·

THE STUDY OF
PLANT LANGUAGES

About this time there was one person whom both the Doctor and I were continually reminded of, and continually wishing for, and that was Long Arrow, the Indian naturalist whom we had met on Spidermonkey Island. To be sure, he had never admitted to the Doctor that he had spoken with plant life. But his knowledge of botany and the natural history of the vegetable kingdom was of such a curious kind we felt that he would have been of great help to us here. Long Arrow, the son of Golden Arrow, never booked a scientific note in his life. How would he—when he was unable to write? Just the same, he could tell you why a certain colored bee visited a certain colored flower, why *that* moth chose *that* shrub to lay its eggs in, why this particular grub attacked the roots of this kind of water plant.

Often of an evening the Doctor and I would speak of him, wondering where he was and what he was doing. When we sailed away from Spidermonkey Island he was left behind. But that would not mean he stayed there. A natural-born tramp who rejoiced in defying the elements and the so-called laws of nature, he could be looked for anywhere in the two American continents.

And again, the Doctor would often refer to my parents. He evidently had a very guilty feeling about them—despite the fact that it was no fault of his that I had stowed away aboard the moth that brought us here. A million and one things filled his mind these days, of course, but whenever there was a letdown, a gap, in the stream of his scientific inquiry, he would come back to the subject.

"Stubbins," he'd say, "you shouldn't have come . . . Yes, yes, I know, you did it for me. But Jacob, your father—and your mother, too—they must be fretting themselves sick about your disappearance. And I am responsible . . . Well, we can't do anything about that now, I suppose. Let's get on with the work."

And then he'd plunge ahead into some new subject and the matter would be dropped—till it bothered him again.

Throughout all our investigations of the moon's vegetable kingdom we could not get away from the idea that the animal life was still, for some unknown reason, steering clear of us. By night, when we were settling down to sleep, we'd often get the impression that huge moths, butterflies, or beetles were flying or crawling near us.

We made quite sure of this once or twice by jumping out of our beds and seeing a giant shadow

HUGH LOFTING

"Seeing a giant shadow disappear into the gloom"

disappear into the gloom. Yet never could we get near enough to distinguish what the creatures were, before they escaped beyond the range of sight. But that they had come—whatever they were—to keep an eye on us seemed quite certain. Also, that all of them were winged. The Doctor had a theory that the lighter gravity of the moon had encouraged the development of wings to a much greater extent than it had on the earth.

And again, those tracks of the strange giant man.

They were always turning up in the most unexpected places. I believe that if the Doctor had allowed Polynesia and Chee-Chee complete liberty to follow them, the enormous human would have been run down in a very short time. But John Dolittle still seemed anxious to keep his family together. I imagine that with his curiously good instinctive judgment he feared an attempt to separate us. And in any case, of course, both Chee-Chee and Polynesia were quite invaluable in a tight place. They were neither of them heavy-weight fighters, it is true; but their usefulness as scouts and guides was enormous. I have often heard John Dolittle say that he would sooner have that monkey or the parrot Polynesia with him in foreign countries than he would the escort of a dozen regiments.

With some of our experimental work we wandered off long distances into the heathlands to see what we could do with the gorgeous flowering shrubs that thronged the rolling downs; and often we followed the streams many miles to study the gigantic lilies that swayed their stately heads over the sedgy banks.

And little by little, our very arduous labors began to be repaid.

I was quite astonished when I came to realize how well the Doctor had prepared for this expedition. Shortly after he decided that he would set to work on the investigation of this supposed language of the plants, he told me we would have to go back and fetch the remainder of our baggage, which we had left at the point of our first arrival.

So the following morning, bright and early, he,

Chee-Chee, and I set out to retrace our steps. Polynesia was left behind. The Doctor told none of us why he did this, but we decided afterward that, as usual, he knew what he was doing.

It was a long and hard trip. It took us a day and a half going there and two days coming back with the load of the baggage. At our original landing place we again found many tracks of the giant human, and other strange marks on the sands about our baggage dump that told us that here, too, curious eyes had been trying to find out things without being seen.

A closer examination of the tracks made by the giant human in these parts where they were especially clear told the Doctor that his right-leg stride was considerably longer than his left. The mysterious Moon Man evidently walked with a limp. But with such a stride he would clearly be a very formidable creature, anyway.

When we got back and started unpacking the bundles and boxes that had been left behind, I saw, as I have already said, how well the Doctor had prepared for his voyage. He seemed to have brought everything that he could possibly need for the trip: hatchets, wire, nails, files, a handsaw, all the things we couldn't get on the moon. It was so different from his ordinary preparations for a voyage—which hardly ever consisted of more than the little black bag and the clothes he stood in.

As usual, he rested only long enough to get a few mouthfuls of food before he set to work. There seemed to be a dozen different apparatuses he wanted to set up at once, some for the testing of

"He seemed to have brought everything he could need"

sound, others for vibrations, etc., etc. With the aid of a saw and an ax and a few other tools, half a dozen small huts had sprung up in an hour around our camp.

· The Tenth Chapter ·
THE MAGELLAN OF THE MOON

Laying aside for the present all worry on the score of why he had been summoned to the moon —of why the animal kingdom continued to treat us with suspicion, of why the giant human so carefully kept out of our way, the Doctor now plunged into the study of plant languages, heart and soul.

He was always happy so, working like a demon, snatching his meals and his sleep here and there, when he thought of such earthly matters. It was a most exhausting time for the rest of us, keeping pace with this firebrand of energy when he got on an interesting scent. And yet it was well worthwhile, too. In one and a half days he had established the fact that the trees *did* converse with one another by means of branch gestures. But that was only the first step. Copying and practicing, he rigged himself up like a tree and talked in the glade—after a fashion—with these centuries-old denizens of the jungle.

From that he learned still more—that language, of

a kind, was carried on by using other means—by scents given out, in a definite way—short or long perfumes, like a regular Morse code; by the tones of wind-song, when branches were set to the right angle to produce certain notes; and many other odd, strange means.

Every night by bedtime, I was nearly dead from the strain and effort of taking notes in those everlasting books, of which he seemed to have brought an utterly inexhaustible supply.

Chee-Chee looked after the feeding of us—thank goodness! Or I fear we would easily have starved to death, if overwork itself hadn't killed us. Every three hours the faithful little monkey would come to us wherever we were at the moment with his messes of strange vegetables and fruits and a supply of good, clean drinking water.

As official recorder of the expedition (a job of which I was very proud, even if it was hard work) I had to write down all the Doctor's calculations as well as his natural-history notes. I have already told you something of temperature, air pressure, time, and whatnot. A further list of them would have included the calculation of distance traveled. This was quite difficult. The Doctor had brought with him a pedometer (a little instrument that when carried in the pocket tells you from the number of strides made, how many miles you've walked). But in the moon, with the changed gravity, a pace was quite different from that usual on the earth. And what is more, it never stayed the same. When the ground sloped downward it was natural to spring a step that quite

HUGH LOFTING

"The faithful monkey would come to us every three hours
with his strange vegetables"

possibly measured six or seven feet—this with no out-
of-the-way effort at all. And even on the up grade one
quite frequently used a stride that was far greater
than in ordinary walking.

It was about this time that the Doctor first spoke of
making a tour of the moon. Magellan, you will remember, was the first to sail around our world. And
it was a very great feat. The earth contains more water area than land. The moon, on the contrary, we

"It was natural to spring a step
that measured six or seven feet"

soon saw, had more dry land than water. There were
no big oceans. Lakes and chains of lakes were all the
water area we saw. To complete a round trip of this
world would therefore be harder, even though it was
shorter, than the voyage that Magellan made.

It was on this account that the Doctor was so particular about my keeping a strict record of the miles
we traveled. As to direction, we had not as yet been
so careful about maintaining a perfectly straight line.

It was by no means easy, for one thing; and for another, the subjects we wished to study, such as tree music, tracks, water supply, rock formation, etc., often led us off toward every quarter of the compass. When I say the *compass* I mean something a little different from the use of that word in earthly geography. As I have told you, the magnetic compass that John Dolittle had brought with him from Puddleby did not behave in a helpful manner at all. Something else must be found to take its place.

John Dolittle, as usual, went after that problem with energy. He was an excellent mathematician, and one afternoon he sat down with a notebook and the nautical almanac and worked out tables that should tell him, from the stars, where he was and in what direction he was going. It was curious, that strange sense of comfort we drew from the stars. They, the heavenly bodies that from the earth seemed the remotest, most distant, unattainable, and strangest of objects, here suddenly became friendly—because, I suppose, they were the only things that really stayed the same. The stars, as we saw them from the moon, were precisely like the stars we had seen from the earth. The fact that they were countless billions of miles away made no difference. For us they were something that we had seen before and knew.

It was while we were at work on devising some contrivance to take the place of the compass that we made the discovery of the explosive wood. The Doctor, after trying many things by which he hoped to keep a definite direction, had suddenly said one day,

HUGH LOFTING

"We rigged up weather vanes"

"Why, Stubbins, I have it. The wind! It always blows steady—and probably from precisely the same quarter or, at all events, with a regular, calculable change, most likely. Let us test it and see."

So right away we set to work to make various wind-testing devices. We rigged up weather vanes from long streamers of light bark. And then John Dolittle hit upon the idea of smoke.

"That is something," said he, "if we only place it properly, that will warn us by smell if the wind changes. And in the meantime we can carry on our studies of the animal kingdom and its languages."

So without further ado we set to work to build fires —or, rather, large smoke smudges—that should tell us how reliable our wind would be if depended on for a source of direction.

· The Eleventh Chapter ·

WE PREPARE TO
CIRCLE THE MOON

We went to a lot of trouble working out how we could best place these fires so that they should give us the most satisfactory results. First of all, we decided with much care on the exact position where we would build them. Mostly they were on bare knolls or shoulders, where they couldn't spread to the underbrush and start a bushfire. Then came the question of fuel: What would be the best wood to build them of?

There were practically no dead trees, as I have said. The only thing to do, then, was to cut some timber down and let it dry.

This we proceeded to do but did not get very far with it before the Doctor suddenly had qualms of conscience. Trees that could talk could, one would suppose, also *feel*. The thought was dreadful. We hadn't even the courage to ask the trees about it—yet. So we fell back upon gathering fallen twigs and small branches. This made the work heavier still because,

"Mostly they were on bare knolls"

of course, we needed a great deal of fuel to have fires big enough to see and smell for any distance.

After a good deal of discussion we decided that this was a thing that couldn't be hurried. A great deal de-. pended on its success. It was a nuisance, truly, but we had just got to be patient. So we went back into the junglelands and set to work on getting out various samples of woods to try.

It took a longish time, for the Doctor and myself were the only ones who could do this work. Chee-

Chee tried to help by gathering twigs; but the material we most needed was wood large enough to last a fair time.

Well, we harvested several different kinds. Some wouldn't burn at all when we tried them. Others, we found, were pretty fair burners but not smoky enough.

With about the fifth kind of wood, I think it was, that we tested out, we nearly had a serious accident. Fire seemed to be (outside of the traces we had found of the smoke-signal apparatus) a thing quite unusual in the moon. There were no traces of forest burnings anywhere, so far as we had explored. It was, therefore, with a good deal of fear and caution that we struck matches to test out our fuel.

About dusk one evening the Doctor set a match to a sort of fern wood (something like a bamboo) and he narrowly escaped a bad burning. The stuff flared up like gunpowder.

We took him off, Chee-Chee and I, and examined him. We found he had suffered no serious injuries, though he had had a very close shave. His hands were somewhat blistered, and he told us what to get out of the little black bag to relieve the inflammation.

We had all noticed that as the wood flared up it sent off dense masses of white smoke. And for hours after the explosion clouds of heavy fumes were still rolling round the hills near us.

When we had the Doctor patched up he told us he was sure that we had stumbled by accident on the fuel that had been used for making the smoke signals we had seen from Puddleby.

"But, my goodness, Doctor," said I, "what an immense bonfire it must have been to be visible all that distance! Thousands of tons of the stuff, surely, must have been piled together to make a smudge that could be seen that far."

"And who could have made it?" put in Chee-Chee.

For a moment there was silence. Then Polynesia spoke the thought that was in my mind—and I imagine in the Doctor's, too.

"The man who made those torches," said she quietly, "could move an awful lot of timber in one day, I'll warrant."

"You mean you think it was *he* who sent the signals?" asked Chee-Chee, his funny little eyes staring wide open with astonishment.

"Why not?" said Polynesia. Then she lapsed into silent contemplation and no further questioning from Chee-Chee could get a word out of her.

"Well," said the monkey at last, "if he *did* send it, that would look as though he were responsible for the whole thing. It must have been he who sent the moth down to us—who needed the Doctor's assistance and presence here."

He looked toward John Dolittle for an answer to this suggestion. But the Doctor, like Polynesia, didn't seem to have anything to say.

Well, in spite of our little mishap, our wood tests with smoke were extremely successful. We found that the wind as a direction pointer could certainly be relied on for three or four days at a time.

"Of course, Stubbins," said the Doctor, "we will have to test again before we set off on our round trip.

HUGH LOFTING

" 'You mean you think it was he who sent the signals?' "

It may be that the breeze, while blowing in one pre-
vailing direction now, may change after a week or so.
Also, we will have to watch it that the mountain
ranges don't deflect the wind's course and so lead us
astray. But from what we have seen so far, I feel
pretty sure that we have here something to take the
place of the compass."

I made one or two attempts later, when Polynesia
and Chee-Chee were out of earshot, to discover what
John Dolittle thought about this idea that it had

" 'I don't know, Stubbins,' said he, frowning"

really been the Moon Man who had brought us here, and not the animal kingdom. I felt that possibly he might talk more freely to me alone on the subject than he had been willing to with all of us listening. But he was strangely untalkative.

"I don't know, Stubbins," said he, frowning. "I really don't know. To tell the truth, my mind is not occupied with that problem now—at all events, not as a matter for immediate decision. This field of the lunar vegetable kingdom is something that could take

up the attention of a hundred naturalists for a year or
two. I feel we have only scratched the surface. As we
go forward into the unknown areas of the moon's
farther side, we are liable to make discoveries of—
well, er—who can tell? When the Moon Man and the
animal kingdom make up their minds that they want
to get in touch with us, I suppose we shall hear from
them. In the meantime, we have our work to do—
more than we can do . . . Gracious, I wish I had a
whole staff with me—surveyors, cartographers, ge-
ologists, and the rest! Think of it! Here we are, messing our way along across a new world—and we don't
even know where we are! I think I have a vague idea
of the line we have followed. And I've tried to keep a
sort of chart of our march. But I should be making
maps, Stubbins, real maps, showing all the peaks, valleys, streams, lakes, plateaus, and everything. Dear,
dear! Well, we must do the best we can."

· The Twelfth Chapter ·

THE VANITY LILIES

Of course, on a globe larger than that of the moon we could never have done as well as we did. When you come to think of it, one man, a boy, a monkey, and a parrot, as a staff for the exploration of a whole world, makes the expedition sound, to say the least, absurd.

We did not realize, any of us, when we started out from our first landing that we were going to make a circular trip of the moon's globe. It just worked out that way. To begin with, we were expecting every hour that some part of the animal kingdom would come forward into the open. But it didn't. And still we went on. Then this language of the trees and flowers came up and got the Doctor going on one of his fever-heat investigations. That carried us still farther. We always took great care when departing from one district for an excursion of any length to leave landmarks behind us, camps or dumps, so that we could

"We always took care to leave landmarks behind us"

find our way back to food and shelter if we should get caught in a tight place.

In this sort of feeling our way forward, Polynesia was most helpful. The Doctor used to let her off regularly to fly ahead of us and bring back reports. That gave us some sort of idea of what we should prepare for. Then, in addition to that, the Doctor had brought with him several small pocket surveying instruments with which he marked on his chart roughly the points at which we changed course to any considerable extent.

In the earlier stages of our trip we had felt we must keep in touch with the first fruit section we had met with, in order to have a supply of vegetables and fruits to rely on for food. But we soon discovered, from Polynesia's scouting reports, that other wooded sections lay ahead of us. To these we sent Chee-Chee, the expert, to investigate. And when he returned and told us that they contained even a better diet than those farther back, we had no hesitation in leaving our old haunts and venturing still farther into the mysteries of the moon's farther side.

The Doctor's progress with the language of the trees and plants seemed to improve with our penetration into the interior. Many times we stopped and pitched camp for four or five days, while he set up some new apparatus and struggled with fresh problems in plant language. It seemed to grow easier and easier for him all the time. Certainly the plant life became more elaborate and lively. By this time we were all grown more accustomed to strange things in the vegetable kingdom. And even to my unscientific eyes it was quite evident that here the flowers and bushes were communicating with one another with great freedom and in many different ways.

I shall never forget our first meeting with the vanity lilies, as the Doctor later came to call them. Great gaudy blooms they were, on long, slender stems that swayed and moved in groups like people whispering and gossiping at a party. When we came in sight of them for the first time, they were more or less mo-

HUGH LOFTING

"Certainly the plant life became more elaborate and lively"

tionless. But as we approached, the movement among them increased as though they were disturbed by, or interested in, our coming.

I think they were, beyond all question, the most beautiful flowers I have ever seen. The wind, regular as ever, had not changed. But the heads of these great masses of plants got so agitated as we drew near that the Doctor decided he would halt the expedition and investigate.

We pitched camp as we called it—a very simple

business in the moon because we did not have to raise tents or build a fire. It was really only a matter of unpacking, getting out the food to eat and the bedding to sleep in.

We were pretty weary after a full day's march. Beyond the lily beds (which lay in a sort of marsh) we could see a new jungle district with more strange trees and flowering creepers.

After a short and silent supper, we lay down and pulled the covers over us. The music of the forest grew louder as darkness increased. It seemed almost as though the whole vegetable world was remarking on these visitors who had invaded their home.

And then, above the music of the woods, we'd hear the drone of flying while we dropped off to sleep. Some of the giant insects were hovering near, as usual, to keep an eye on these creatures from another world.

I think that of all our experiences with the plant life of the moon that with the vanity lilies was perhaps the most peculiar and the most thrilling. In about two days the Doctor had made extraordinary strides in his study of this language. That, he explained to me, was due more to the unusual intelligence of this species and its willingness to help than to his own efforts. But, of course, if he had not already done considerable work with the trees and bushes, it is doubtful if the lilies could have gotten in touch with him as quickly as they did.

By the end of the third day Chee-Chee, Polynesia, and I were all astonished to find that John Dolittle was actually able to carry on conversation with these

HUGH LOFTING

"The flowers would be about eighteen inches across"

flowers. And this with the aid of very little apparatus. He had now discovered that the vanity lilies spoke among themselves largely by the movement of their blossoms. They used different means of communication with species of plants and trees other than their own—and also (we heard later) in talking with birds and insects; but among themselves the swaying of the flower heads was the common method of speech.

The lilies, when seen in great banks, presented a very gorgeous and wonderful appearance. The flowers would be, I should judge, about eighteen inches across, trumpet-shaped, and brilliantly colored. The background was a soft cream tone and on this great blotches of violet and orange were grouped around a jet-black tongue in the center. The leaves were a deep olive-green.

But it was that extraordinary look of alive intelligence that was the most uncanny thing about them. No one, no matter how little he knew of natural history in general or of the moon's vegetable kingdom, could see those wonderful flowers without immediately being arrested by this peculiar character. You felt at once that you were in the presence of people rather than plants; and to talk with them, or to try to, seemed the most natural thing in the world.

I filled up two of those numerous notebooks of the Doctor's on his conversations with the vanity lilies. Often he came back to these flowers later, when he wanted further information about the moon's vegetable kingdom. For, as he explained to us, it was in this species that plant life—so far as it was known on either the moon or the earth—had reached its highest point of development.

· The Thirteenth Chapter ·
THE FLOWER OF MANY SCENTS

Another peculiar thing that baffled us completely, when we first came into the marshy regions of the vanity lilies' home, was the variety of scents that assailed our noses. For a mile or so around the locality there was no other flower visible; the whole of the marsh seemed to have been taken up by the lilies, and nothing else intruded on their domain. Yet at least half a dozen perfumes were distinct and clear. At first, we thought that perhaps the wind might be bringing us scents from other plants either in the jungle or the flowering heathlands. But the direction of the breeze was such that it could only come over the sandy desert areas and was not likely to bring perfumes as strong as this.

It was the Doctor who first hit upon the idea that possibly the lily could give off more than one scent at will. He set to work to find out right away. And it took no more than a couple of minutes to convince him that it could. He said he was sorry he had not got

87

Jip with him. Jip's expert sense of smell would have been very useful here. But for ordinary purposes it required nothing more delicate than an average human's nose to tell that this flower, when John Dolittle had communicated the idea to it, was clearly able to give out at least half a dozen different smells as it wished.

The majority of these perfumes were extremely agreeable. But there were one or two that nearly knocked you down. It was only after the Doctor had asked the lilies about this gift of theirs that they sent forth obnoxious ones in demonstrating all the scents that they could give out. Chee-Chee just fainted away at the first sample. It was like some deadly gas. It got into your eyes and made them run. The Doctor and I escaped suffocation only by flight—carrying the body of the unconscious monkey along with us.

The vanity lilies, seeing what distress they had caused, immediately threw out the most soothing, lovely scent I have ever smelled. Clearly they were anxious to please us and cultivate our acquaintance. Indeed it turned out later from their conversation with the Doctor (which I took down word for word) that, in spite of being a stationary part of the moon's landscape, they had heard of John Dolittle, the great naturalist, and had been watching for his arrival many days. They were, in fact, the first creatures in our experience of the moon that made us feel we were among friends.

I think I could not do better, in trying to give you an idea of the Doctor's communication with the vegetable kingdom of the moon, than to set down from

"Chee-Chee just fainted away at the first sample"

my diary, word for word, some parts of the conversation between him and the vanity lilies, as he translated them to me for dictation at the time. Even so, there are many I am sure who will doubt the truth of the whole idea: that a man could talk with the flowers. But with them I am not so concerned. Anyone who had followed John Dolittle through the various stages of animal, fish, and insect languages would not, I feel certain, find it very strange, when the great man did at last come in touch with plant life of unusual intelligence, that he should be able to converse with it.

On looking over my diary of those eventful days the scene of that occasion comes up visibly before my eyes. It was about an hour before dusk—that is, the slight dimming of the pale daylight that preceded a half darkness, the nearest thing to real night we ever saw on the moon. The Doctor, as we left the camp, called back over his shoulder to me to bring an extra notebook along, as he expected to make a good deal of progress tonight. I armed myself therefore with three extra books and followed him out.

Halting about twenty paces in front of the lily beds (we had camped back several hundred yards from them after they had nearly suffocated Chee-Chee), the Doctor squatted on the ground and began swaying his head from side to side. Immediately the lilies began moving their heads in answer, swinging, nodding, waving, and dipping.

"Are you ready, Stubbins?" asked John Dolittle.

"Yes, Doctor," said I, making sure my pencil point would last a while.

"Good," said he. "Put it down":

The Doctor: Do you like this stationary life—I mean, living in the same place all the time, unable to move?

The lilies (Several of them seemed to answer in chorus): Why, yes—of course. Being stationary doesn't bother us. We hear about all that is going on.

The Doctor: From whom, what, do you hear it?

" 'Are you ready, Stubbins?' "

The lilies: Well, the other plants, the bees, the birds, bring us news of what is happening.

The Doctor: Oh, do you communicate with the bees and the birds?

The lilies: Why, certainly, of course!

The Doctor: Yet the bees and the birds are species different from your own.

The lilies: Quite true, but the bees come to us for honey. And the birds come to sit among our leaves —especially the warblers—and they sing and talk and tell us of what is happening in the world. What more would you want?

The Doctor: Oh, quite so, quite so. I didn't mean you should be discontented. But don't you ever want to move, to travel?

The lilies: Good gracious, no! What's the use of all this running about? After all, there's no place like home—provided it's a good one. It's a pleasant life we lead—and very safe. The folks who rush around are always having accidents, breaking legs and so forth. Those troubles can't happen to us. We sit still and watch the world go by. We chat sometimes among ourselves and then there is always the gossip of the birds and the bees to entertain us.

The Doctor: And you really understand the language of the birds and bees! You astonish me.

The lilies: Oh, perfectly—and of the beetles and moths, too.

It was at about this point in our first recorded conversation that we made the astonishing discovery that the vanity lilies could *see.* The light, as I have told you, was always somewhat dim on the moon. The Doctor, while he was talking, suddenly decided he would like a smoke. He asked the lilies if they objected to the fumes of tobacco. They said they did not know because they had never had any experience of it. So the Doctor said he would light his pipe and if they did not like it he would stop.

So, taking a box of matches from his pocket, he struck a light. We had not fully realized before how soft and gentle was the light of the moon until that

HUGH LOFTING

"He struck a light"

match flared up. It is true that in testing our woods for smoke fuel we had made much larger blazes. But then, I suppose we had been more intent on the results of our experiments than on anything else. Now, as we noticed the lilies suddenly draw back their heads and turn aside from the flare, we saw that the extra illumination of a mere match had made a big difference to the ordinary daylight they were accustomed to.

· The Fourteenth Chapter ·
MIRRORS FOR FLOWERS

When the Doctor noticed how the lilies shrank away from the glow of the matches, he became greatly interested in this curious unexpected effect that the extra light had had on them.

"Why, Stubbins," he whispered, "they could not have felt the heat. We were too far away. If it is the glare that made them draw back, it must be that they have some organs so sensitive to light that quite possibly *they can see!* I must find out about this."

Thereupon he began questioning the lilies again to discover how much they could tell him of their sense of vision. He shot his hand out and asked them if they knew what movement he had made. Every time (though they had no idea of what he was trying to find out) they told him precisely what he had done. Then, going close to one large flower, he passed his hand all around it, and the blossom turned its head and faced the moving hand all the way around the circle.

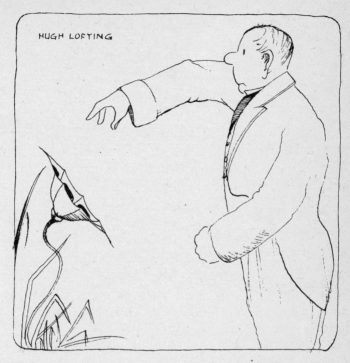

"He passed his hand all around it"

There was no doubt in our minds whatever, when we had finished our experiments, that the vanity lilies could, in their own way, see—though where the machinery called "eyes" was placed in their anatomy we could not as yet discover.

The Doctor spent hours and days trying to solve this problem. But, he told me, he met with very little success. For a while he was forced to the conclusion (since he could not find in the flowers any eyes such as we knew) that what he had taken for a sense of vision was only some other sense, highly developed, that produced the same results as seeing.

"After all, Stubbins," said he, "just because we ourselves have only five senses, it doesn't follow that other creatures can't have more. It has long been supposed that certain birds had a sixth sense. Still, the way those flowers feel light, can tell colors, movement, and form, makes it look very much as though they had found a way of seeing—even if they haven't got eyes . . . Humph! Yes, one might quite possibly see with other things besides eyes."

Going through his baggage that night after our day's work was done, the Doctor discovered among his papers an illustrated catalogue that had somehow got packed by accident. John Dolittle, always a devoted gardener, had catalogues sent to him from nearly every seed merchant and nurseryman in England.

"Why, Stubbins!" he cried, turning over the pages of gorgeous annuals in high glee. "Here's a chance: If those lilies can see, we can test them with this—pictures of flowers in color!"

The next day he interviewed the vanity lilies with the catalogue, and his work was rewarded with very good results. Taking the brightly colored pictures of petunias, chrysanthemums, and hollyhocks, he held them in a good light before the faces of the lilies. Even Chee-Chee and I could see at once that this caused quite a sensation. The great trumpet-shaped blossoms swayed downward and forward on their slender stems to get a closer view of the pages. Then

"He held them before the lilies"

they turned to one another as though in critical conversation.

Later, the Doctor interpreted to me the comments they had made, and I wrote them among the notes. They seemed most curious to know *who* these flowers were. They spoke of them (or, rather, of their species) in a peculiarly personal way. This was one of the first occasions when we got some idea or glimpses of lunar *vegetable society,* as the Doctor later came to call it. It almost seemed as though these

beautiful creatures were surprised, like human la-
dies, at the portraits displayed and wanted to know
all about these foreign beauties and the lives they led.

This interest in personal appearance on the part of
the lilies was, as a matter of fact, what originally led
the Doctor to call their species the *vanity lily*. In their
own strange tongue they questioned him for hours
and hours about these outlandish flowers whose pictures he had shown them. They seemed very disap-
pointed when he told them the actual size of most
earthly flowers. But they seemed a little pleased that
their sisters of the other world could not, at least,
compete with them in that. They were also much
mystified when John Dolittle explained to them that,
with us, no flowers or plants (so far as was known)
had communicated with Man, birds, or any other
members of the animal kingdom.

Questioning them further on this point of personal
appearance, the Doctor was quite astonished to find
to what an extent it occupied their attention. He
found that they always tried to get near water so that
they could see their own reflections in the surface.
They got terribly upset if some bee or bird came
along and disturbed the pollen powder on their gorgeous petals or set awry the angle of their pistils.

The Doctor talked to various groups and individu-
als; and in the course of his investigations he came
across several plants who, while they had begun their
peaceful lives close to a nice pool or stream that they
could use as a mirror, had sadly watched while the
water had dried up and left nothing but sunbaked
clay for them to look into.

So, then and there, John Dolittle halted his questioning of the vanity lilies for a spell, while he set to work to provide these unfortunates, whose natural mirrors had dried up, with something in which they could see themselves.

We had no regular looking glasses of course, beyond the Doctor's own shaving mirror, which he could not very well part with. But from the provisions, we dug out various caps and bottoms of preserved fruits and sardine tins. These we polished with clay and rigged up on sticks so that the lilies could see themselves in them.

"It is a fact, Stubbins," said the Doctor, "that the natural tendency is always to grow the way you want to grow. These flowers have a definite, conscious idea of what they consider beautiful and what they consider ugly. These contrivances we have given them, poor though they are, will therefore have a decided effect on their evolution."

That is one of the pictures from our adventures in the moon that always stands out in my memory: the vanity lilies, happy in the possession of their new mirrors, turning their heads this way and that to see how their pollen-covered petals glowed in the soft light, swaying with the wind, comparing, whispering, and gossiping.

I truly believe that if other events had not interfered, the Doctor would have been occupied quite contentedly with his study of these very advanced plants for months. And there was certainly a great deal to be learned from them. They told him, for

"These we rigged up on sticks"

instance, of another species of lily that he later came to call the *poison lily* or *vampire lily*. This flower liked to have plenty of room and it obtained it by sending out deadly scents (much more serious in their effects than those unpleasant ones that the vanities used), and nothing around about it could exist for long.

Following the directions given by the vanity lilies, we finally ran some of these plants down and actually conversed with them—though we were in continual fear that they would be displeased with us and might any moment send out their poisonous gases to destroy us.

From still other plants that the vanities directed us to, the Doctor learned a great deal about what he called "methods of propagating." Certain bushes, for example, could crowd out weeds and other shrubs by increasing the speed of their growth at will and by spreading their seed abroad several times a year.

In our wanderings, looking for these latter plants, we came across great fields of the moon bells flourishing and growing under natural conditions. And very gorgeous indeed they looked, acres and acres of brilliant orange. The air was full of their invigorating perfume. The Doctor wondered if we would see anything of our giant moth near these parts. But though we hung about for several hours, we saw very few signs of insect life.

· The Fifteenth Chapter ·
MAKING NEW CLOTHES

I don't understand it at all," John Dolittle muttered. "What reason at least can the moth who brought us here have for keeping out of our way?"

"His reasons may not be his own," murmured Polynesia.

"What do you mean?" asked the Doctor.

"Well," said she, "others may be keeping him—and the rest—away from us."

"You mean the Moon Man?" said John Dolittle.

But to this Polynesia made no reply and the subject was dropped.

"That isn't the thing that's bothering me so much," said Chee-Chee.

There was a pause. And before he went on I know that all of us were quite sure what was in his mind.

"It's our getting back home," he said at last. "Getting here was done for us by these moon folks—for whatever reason they had. But we'd stand a mighty poor chance of ever reaching the earth again if they're going to stand off and leave us to ourselves to get back."

Another short spell of silence—during which we all did a little serious and gloomy thinking.

"Oh, well," said the Doctor, "come, come! Don't let's bother about the stiles till we reach them. After all, we don't know for certain that these—er—whoever it is—are definitely unfriendly to us. They may have reasons of their own for working slowly. You must remember that we are just as strange and outlandish to them as they and their whole world are to us. We mustn't let any idea of that kind become a nightmare. We have only been here, let's see, not much over two weeks. It is a pleasant land and there is lots to be learned. The vegetable kingdom is clearly well disposed toward us. And if we give them time, I'm sure that the—er—others will be too, in the end."

Another matter that came up about this time was the effect of moon food on ourselves. Polynesia was the first to remark upon it.

"Tommy," said she one day, "you seem to be getting enormously tall—and fat, aren't you?"

"Er—am I?" said I. "Well, I *had* noticed my belt seemed a bit tight. But I thought it was just ordinary growing."

"And the Doctor, too," the parrot went on. "I'll swear he's bigger—unless my eyesight is getting queer."

"Well, we can soon prove that," said John Dolittle. "I know my height exactly—five feet two and a half. I have a two-foot ruler in the baggage. I'll measure myself against a tree right away."

HUGH LOFTING

" 'Tommy, you seem to be getting enormously tall' "

When the Doctor had accomplished this he was astonished to find that his height had increased some
three inches since he had been on the moon. Of what
my own had been before I landed, I was not so sure,
but measurement made it, too, a good deal more than
I had thought it. And as to my waistline, there was no
doubt that it had grown enormously. Even Chee-
Chee, when we came to look at him, seemed larger
and heavier. Polynesia was, of course, so small that it

"His height had increased some three inches"

would need an enormous increase in her figure to make difference enough to see.

But there was no question at all that the rest of us had grown considerably since we had been here.

"Well," said the Doctor, "I suppose it is reasonable enough. All the vegetable and insect world here is tremendously much larger than corresponding species in our own world. Whatever helped them to grow—climate, food, atmosphere, air pressure, etc.— should make us do the same. There is a great deal in this for the investigation of biologists and physiologists. I suppose the long seasons—or almost no seasons at all, you might say—and the other things that contribute to the long life of the animal and vegetable species would lengthen our lives to hundreds of years if we lived here continually. You know, when I was talking to the vampire lilies the other day they told me that even cut flowers—which, with them, would mean of course only blossoms that were broken off by the wind or accident—live perfectly fresh for weeks and even months, provided they get a little moisture. That accounts for the moon bells, which the moth brought down with him, lasting so well in Puddleby. No, we've got to regard this climate as something entirely different from the earth's. There is no end to the surprises it may spring on us yet. Oh, well, I suppose we will shrink back to our ordinary size when we return home. Still, I hope we don't grow too gigantic. My waistcoat feels most uncomfortably tight already. It's funny we didn't notice it earlier. But, goodness knows, we have had enough to keep our attention occupied."

It had been, indeed, this absorbing interest in all the new things that the moon presented to our eyes that had prevented us from noticing our own changed condition. The following few days, however, our growth went forward at such an amazing pace that I began seriously to worry about it. My clothes were literally splitting and the Doctor's also. Finally, taking counsel on the matter, we proceeded to look into what means this world offered of making new ones.

Luckily, the Doctor, while he knew nothing about tailoring, did know something about the natural history of those plants and materials that supply clothes and textile fabrics for Man.

"Let me see," said he one afternoon when we had decided that almost everything we wore had become too small to be kept any longer. "Cotton is out of the question. The spinning would take too long, even if we had any, to say nothing of the weaving. Linen? No, likewise. I haven't seen anything that looked like a flax plant. About all that remains is root fiber, though heaven help us if we have to wear that kind of material next to our skins! Well, we must investigate and see what we can find."

With the aid of Chee-Chee, we searched the woods. It took us several days to discover anything suitable, but finally we did. It was an odd-looking swamp tree whose leaves were wide and soft. We found that when these were dried in the proper way they kept a certain pliability without becoming stiff or brittle. And yet they were tough enough to be sewn without tearing. Chee-Chee and Polynesia supplied us with the thread we needed. This they obtained from certain vine tendrils—very fine—that they shredded and twisted into yarn. Then one evening we set to work and cut out our new suits.

"Better make them large enough," said the Doctor, waving a pair of scissors over our rock worktable. "Goodness only knows how soon we'll outgrow them."

We had a lot of fun at one another's expense when

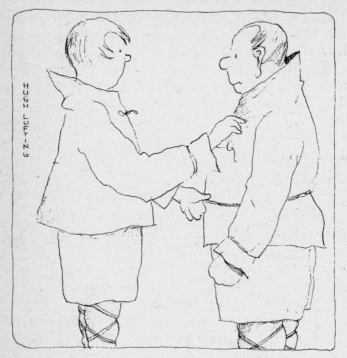

" 'We look like a family of Robinson Crusoes' "

at length the suits were completed and we tried them on.

"We look like a family of Robinson Crusoes," said John Dolittle. "No matter: They will serve our purpose. Any port in a storm."

For underwear we cut up all we had and made one garment out of two or three. We were afraid as yet to try our new tailoring next to the skin. Luckily, we only had to provide for a very mild climate.

"Now what about footwear?" said I when I had my coat and trousers on. "My shoes are all split across the top."

"That part is easy," said Chee-Chee. "I know a tree in the jungle that I found when hunting for fruits. The bark strips off easily and you can cut it into sandals that will last quite a while. The only hard part will be plaiting thongs strong enough to keep them in place on your feet."

He guided us to the tree he had spoken of, and we soon had outfitted ourselves with footgear that would last us at least a week.

"Good!" said the Doctor. "Now we need not worry about clothes, for a while, anyway, and can give our attention to more serious matters."

· The Sixteenth Chapter ·

MONKEY MEMORIES
OF THE MOON ·

It was when we were on our way to visit still another new kind of plant that the subject of the moon's early history came up again in conversation. The Doctor had heard of a "whispering vine" that used, as a method of conversation, the rattling or whispering of its leaves.

"Do you remember, Chee-Chee?" the Doctor asked, "if your grandmother ever spoke, in her stories of very ancient times, of any peculiar or extraordinary plants or trees?"

"I don't think so, Doctor," he replied. "My grandmother in her talks of the time before there was a moon kept pretty much to animals and people. She hardly ever mentioned the trees or vegetable world, except to say of this country or that, that it was heavily wooded or bare and desert. Why?"

"Well, of course, in my mind there is no doubt that the moon was once a part of the earth, as many scientists believe. And, if so, I am wondering why we do not see more plants and trees of our own home kinds here."

"Well, but we have, Doctor," said Polynesia. "How about the asparagus forests?"

"Quite so," said the Doctor. "There have been many that reminded one of earthly species in their shapes, even if they have grown into giants here. But this speech among plants and trees—and other evidences of social advance and development in the vegetable kingdom—is something so established and accepted here, I am all the time wondering if something like it had not started on the earth long ago—say, in the days before there was a moon. And it was merely because our naturalists were not quick enough to—er —catch on to it, that we supposed there was no means of communication among flowers and trees."

"Let me think," said Chee-Chee, and he held his forehead tightly with both hands.

"No," he said after a while. "I don't recall my grandmother's speaking of things like that at all. I remember in her story of Otho Bludge, the prehistoric artist, that she told us about certain woods he used to make handles for his flint chisels and other tools and household implements. She described the wood, for instance, that he used to make bowls out of for carrying water in. But she never spoke of trees and plants that could talk."

It was about midday and we had halted for lunch on our excursion in search of the whispering vines we had been told of. We were not more than two or three hours' walk from our old base camp. But that,

" 'Let me think,' said Chee-Chee"

with the speed so easy in moon marching, means a
much greater distance than it does on the earth.
From this camp, where the Doctor had set up his apparatus for his special botanical studies, we had now
for nearly a week been making daily expeditions in
search of the various new species that the vanity lilies
had described for us. But we always got back before
nightfall. Well, this noon the Doctor was leaning
back, munching a large piece of yellow yam—a vegetable we got from the edges of the jungle and which

"Leaning back, munching a piece of yellow yam"

we had found so nourishing we had made it almost our chief article of diet.

"Tell me, Chee-Chee," said he, "what was the end of that story about Otho Bludge, the prehistoric artist? It was a most fascinating tale."

"Well, I think I have told you," said Chee-Chee, "pretty nearly all there was to tell. In the days before there was a moon, as Grandmother always began, Otho Bludge was a man alone, a man apart. Making pictures on horn and bone with a stone knife—that was his hobby. His great ambition was to make a picture of Man. But there was no one to draw from, for Otho Bludge was a man alone. One day, when he wished aloud for someone to make a picture from, he saw this beautiful girl—Pippiteepa was her name—kneeling on a rock, waiting for him to make a portrait of her. He made it—the best work he ever did, carved into the flat of a reindeer's antler. About her right ankle she wore a string of blue stone beads. When the picture was finished she started to disappear again into the mountains' evening mist, as mysteriously as she had come. Otho called to her to stay. She was the only human being he had ever seen, besides his own image in the pools. He wanted her company, poor Otho Bludge, the carver of horn, the man apart. But even as she passed into the twilight forever, she cried out to him that she could not stay—for she was of the fairy folk and not of his kin. He rushed to the rock where she had knelt; but all he found was the string of blue stone beads that she had worn about her ankle. Otho, brokenhearted, took them and bound them on his own wrist, where he wore them night and day, hoping always that she would come back.

"There is nothing more. We youngsters used to pester my grandmother for a continuance of the tale. It seemed so sad, so unsatisfying, an ending. But the old lady insisted that that *was* the end. Not long after apparently, Otho Bludge, the carver of horn and the man apart, just disappeared completely, as though the earth had swallowed him up."

"Humph!" muttered the Doctor. "Have you any idea when?"

"No," said the monkey. "You see, even my grandmother's ideas of time and place in these stories she told us were very hazy. She had only had them handed down to her by her parents and grandparents, just as she passed them on to us. But I am pretty sure it was around the time of the great flood. Grandmother used to divide her stories into two periods: those belonging to the days before there was a moon and those that happened after. The name of Otho Bludge, the artist, only came into those before."

"I see," said the Doctor thoughtfully. "But tell me, can you recall anything your grandmother said about the time of the change—I mean, when the one period left off and the other began?"

"Not a very great deal," said Chee-Chee. "It was the same when we questioned her about the flood. That that event had taken place, there was no doubt; but, except for a few details, very little seemed to have been handed down as to how it came about, or of what was going on on the earth at the time or immediately after it. I imagine they were both great catastrophes—perhaps both came together—and such confusion fell upon all creatures that they were far too busy to take notes, and too scattered afterward to keep a very clear picture in their minds. But I do remember that my grandmother said the first night when the moon appeared in the sky some of our monkey ancestors saw a group of men kneeling on a mountaintop worshiping it. They had always been

sun worshipers and were now offering up prayers to
the moon also, saying it must be the sun's wife."

"But," asked the Doctor, "did not Man know that
the moon must have flown off from the earth?"

"That is not very clear," said Chee-Chee. "We often
questioned my grandmother on this point. But there
were certainly some awfully big gaps in her information. It was like a history put together from odd bits
that had been seen from different sides of the earth
and filled in by gossip and hearsay generations after.
It seems that, to begin with, the confusion was terrible. Darkness covered the earth; the noise of a terrible explosion followed; and there was great loss of
life. Then the sea rushed into the hole that had been
made, causing more havoc and destruction still. Man
and beast slunk into caves for shelter or ran wild
across the mountains, or just lay down and covered
their eyes to shut out the dreadful vision. From what
monkey history has to relate, none lived who had actually seen the thing take place. But that I have always doubted. And much later there was a regular
war among mankind when human society had pulled
itself together again sufficiently to get back to something like the old order."

"What was the war about?" asked the Doctor.

"Well, by that time," said Chee-Chee, "Man had
multiplied considerably, and there were big cities everywhere. The war was over the question: Was the
moon a goddess, or was she not? The old sun worshipers said she was the wife or daughter of the sun
and was therefore entitled to adoration. Those who
said the moon had flown off from the flanks of the

"A terrible explosion followed"

earth had given up worshiping the sun. They held that if the earth had the power to shoot off another world like that, that *it* should be adored as the mother earth from which we got everything, and not the sun. They said it showed the earth was the center of all things, since the sun had never shot off children. Then there were others who said that the sun and the new earth should be adored as gods—and yet others that wanted all three—sun and earth and moon—to form a great triangle of almighty power.

The war was a terrible one, men killing one another
in thousands—greatly to the astonishment of the
monkey people. For to us it did not seem that any of
the various parties really *knew* anything for certain
about the whole business."

"Dear, dear," the Doctor muttered as Chee-Chee
ended. "The first religious strife—the first of so many.
What a pity! Just as though it mattered to anyone
what his neighbor believed, so long as he himself led
a sincere and useful life and was happy!"

· The Seventeenth Chapter ·
WE HEAR OF "THE COUNCIL"

This expedition on the trail of the whispering vines proved to be one of the most fruitful and satisfactory of all our excursions.

When we finally arrived at the home of this species, we found it a very beautiful place. It was a rocky gulch hard by the jungle, where a dense curtain of creepers hung down into a sort of pocket precipice with a spring-fed pool at the bottom. In such a place you could imagine fairies dancing in the dusk, wild beasts of the forest sheltering, or outlaws making their headquarters.

With a squawk Polynesia flew up and settled in the hanging tendrils that draped the rock wall. Instantly we saw a general wave of movement go through the vines and a whispering noise broke out that could be plainly heard by any ears. Evidently the vines were somewhat disturbed at this invasion by a bird they did not know. Polynesia, a little upset herself, flew back to us at once.

"It was a rocky gulch"

"Shiver my timbers!" said she in a disgruntled mutter. "This country would give a body the creeps. Those vines actually moved and squirmed like snakes when I took hold of them."

"They are not used to you, Polynesia," laughed the Doctor. "You probably scared them to death. Let us see if we can get into conversation with them."

Here the Doctor's experience with the singing trees came in very helpfully. I noticed as I watched him go to work with what small apparatus he had brought with him that he now seemed much surer of how to begin. And it was indeed a surprisingly short time before he was actually in conversation with them, as though he had almost been talking with them all his life.

Presently he turned to me and spoke almost the thought that was in my mind.

"Stubbins," he said, "the ease with which these plants answer me would almost make me think *they have spoken with a man before!* Look, I can actually make responses with the lips, like ordinary human speech."

He dropped the little contrivance he held in his hands and, hissing softly through his teeth, he gave out a sort of whispered cadence. It was a curious combination between someone humming a tune and hissing a conversational sentence.

Usually it had taken John Dolittle some hours, occasionally some days, to establish a communication with these strange, almost human moon trees good enough to exchange ideas with them. But both Chee-Chee and I grunted with astonishment at the way they instantly responded to his whispered speech. Swinging their leafy tendrils around to meet the breeze at a certain angle, they instantly gave back a humming, hissing message that might have been a repetition of that made by the Doctor himself.

"They say they are glad to see us, Stubbins," he jerked out over his shoulder.

"Why, Doctor," I said, "this is marvelous! You got results right away. I never saw anything like it."

"They have spoken with a man before," he

repeated. "Not a doubt of it. I can tell by the way they — Good gracious, what's this?"

He turned and found Chee-Chee tugging at his left sleeve. I have never seen the poor monkey so overcome with fright. He stuttered and jibbered, but no intelligible sounds came through his chattering teeth.

"Why, Chee-Chee!" said the Doctor. "What is it? What's wrong?"

"Look!" was all he finally managed to gulp.

He pointed down to the margin of the pond lying at the foot of the cliff. We had scaled up to a shelf of rock to get nearer to the vines for convenience. Where the monkey now pointed there was clearly visible in the yellow sand of the pool's beach two enormous footprints such as we had seen by the shores of the lake.

"The Moon Man!" the Doctor whispered. "Well, I was sure of it—that these vines had spoken with a man before. I wonder—"

"Sh!" Polynesia interrupted. "Don't let them see you looking. But when you get a chance, glance up toward the left-hand shoulder of the gulch."

Both the Doctor and I behaved as though we were proceeding with our business of conversing with the vines. Then, pretending I was scratching my ear, I looked up in the direction the parrot had indicated. There I saw several birds. They were trying to keep themselves hidden among the leaves. But there was no doubt that they were there on the watch.

As we turned back to our work an enormous shadow passed over us, shutting off the light of the sun. We looked up, fearing, as anyone would, some

"There was no doubt that they were on the watch"

attack or danger from the air. Slowly, a giant moth of the same kind that had brought us to this mysterious world sailed across the heavens and disappeared.

A general silence fell over us all that must have lasted a good three minutes.

"Well," said the Doctor at length, "if this means that the animal kingdom has decided finally to make our acquaintance, so much the better. Those are the first birds we have seen—and that was the first insect— since our moth left us. Curious, to find the bird life so much smaller than the insect. However, I suppose they will let us know more when they are ready. Meantime, we have plenty to do here. Have you a notebook, Stubbins?"

"Yes, Doctor," said I. "I'm quite prepared whenever you are."

Thereupon the Doctor proceeded with his conversation with the whispering vines and fired off questions and answers so fast that I was kept more than busy noting what he said.

It was indeed, as I have told you, by far the most satisfactory inquiry we had made into the life of the moon, animal or vegetable, up to that time. Because while these vines had not the almost human appearance of the vanity lilies, they did seem to be in far closer touch with the general life of the moon. The Doctor asked them about this warfare that we had heard of from the last plants we had visited—the struggle that occurred when one species of plant wished for more room and had to push away its intruding neighbors. And it was then, for the first time, we heard about the council.

"Oh," said they, "you mustn't get the idea that one species of plant is allowed to make war for its own benefit, regardless of the lives or rights of others. Oh, dear, no! We folk of the moon have long since gotten past that. There was a day when we had constant strife, species against species, plants against plants, birds against insects, and so on. But not anymore."

"Well, how do you manage," asked the Doctor, "when two different species want the same thing?"

"It's all arranged by the council," said the vines.

"Proceeded with his conversation with the vines"

"Er—excuse me," said the Doctor. "I don't quite understand. What council?"

"Well, you see," said the vines, "some hundreds of years ago—that is, of course, well within the memory of most of us, we—"

"Excuse me again," the Doctor interrupted. "Do you mean that most of the plants and insects and birds here have been living several centuries already?"

"Why, certainly," said the whispering vines. "Some,

of course, are older than others. But here on the
moon we consider a plant or a bird or a moth quite
young if he has seen no more than two hundred
years. And there are several trees, and a few members of the animal kingdom, too, whose memories go
back to over a thousand years."

"You don't say!" murmured the Doctor. "I realized,
of course, that your lives were much longer than ours
on the earth, but I had no idea you went as far back
as that. Goodness me! Well, please go on."

"In the old days, then, before we instituted the
council," the vines continued, "there was a terrible
lot of waste and slaughter. They tell of one time when
a species of big lizard overran the whole moon. They
grew so enormous that they ate up almost all the
green stuff there was. No tree or bush or plant got a
chance to bring itself to seeding-time because as soon
as it put out a leaf it was gobbled up by those hungry
brutes. Then the rest of us got together to see what we
could do."

"Er—pardon," said the Doctor. "But how do you
mean, got together? You plants could not move, could
you?"

"Oh, no," said the vines. "We couldn't move. But we
could communicate with the rest—take part in con-
ferences, as it were, by means of messengers—birds
and insects, you know."

"How long ago was that?" asked the Doctor. "I
mean, for how long has the animal and vegetable
world here been able to communicate with one another?"

"Precisely," said the vines, "we can't tell you. Of

HUGH LOFTING

"A species of big lizard overran the moon"

course some sort of communication goes back a perfectly enormous long way, some hundreds of thousands of years. But it was not always as good as it is now. It has been improving all the time. Nowadays it would be impossible for anything of any importance at all to happen in our corner of the moon without its being passed along through plants and trees and insects and birds to every other corner of our globe within a few moments. For instance, we have known almost every movement you and your party have made since you landed in our world."

"Dear me!" muttered the Doctor. "I had no idea. However, please proceed."

"Of course," they went on, "it was not always so. But after the institution of the council, communication and cooperation became much better and continued to grow until it reached its present stage."

· The Eighteenth Chapter ·
THE PRESIDENT

The whispering vines then went on to tell the Doctor in greater detail of that institution that they had vaguely spoken of already, the council. This was apparently a committee or general government made up of members from both the animal and vegetable kingdoms. Its main purpose was to regulate life on the moon in such a way that there should be no more warfare. For example, if a certain kind of shrub wanted more room for expansion, and the territory it wished to take over was already occupied by, we'll say, bullrushes, it was not allowed to thrust out its neighbor without first submitting the case to the council. Or if a certain kind of butterfly wished to feed upon the honey of some flower and was interfered with by a species of bee or beetle, again the argument had to be put to the vote of this all-powerful committee before any action could be taken.

This information explained a great deal that had heretofore puzzled us.

"You see, Stubbins," said the Doctor, "the great size

of almost all life here, the development of intelligence in plant forms, and much more besides, could not possibly have come about if this regulation had not been in force. Our world could learn a lot from the moon, Stubbins—the moon, its own child, whom it presumes to despise! We have no balancing or real protection of life. With us, it is, and always has been, 'dog eat dog.'"

The Doctor shook his head and gazed off into space to where the globe of our mother earth glowed dimly. Just so had I often seen the moon from Puddleby by daylight.

"Yes," he repeated, his manner becoming of a sudden deeply serious, "our world that thinks itself so far advanced has not the wisdom, the foresight, Stubbins, that we have seen here. Fighting, fighting, fighting, always fighting! So it goes on down there with us . . . The 'survival of the fittest'! . . . I've spent my whole life trying to help the animal, the so-called lower forms of life. I don't mean I am complaining. Far from it. I've had a very good time getting in touch with the beasts and winning their friendship. If I had my life over again, I'd do just the same thing. But often, so often, I have felt that in the end it was bound to be a losing game. It is this thing here, this council of life—of life adjustment—that could have saved the day and brought happiness to all."

"Yes, Doctor," said I. "But listen, compared with our world, they have no animal life here at all, so far as we've seen. Only insects and birds. They've no lions or tigers who have to hunt for deer and wild goats to get a living, have they?"

"Where the globe of the earth glowed dimly"

"True, Stubbins—probably true," said he. "But don't forget that that same warfare of species against species goes on in the insect kingdom as well as among the larger carnivora. In another million years from now some scientist may show that the war going on between Man and the housefly today is the most important thing in current history. And besides, who shall say what kind of a creature the tiger was before he took to a diet of meat?"

John Dolittle then turned back to the vines and

asked some further questions. These were mostly about the council—how it worked, of what it was composed, how often it met, etc. And the answers that they gave filled out a picture that we had already half guessed and half seen of life on the moon.

When I come to describe it, I find myself wishing that I were a great poet or, at all events, a great writer. For this moon-world was indeed a land of wondrous rest. Trees that sang, flowers that could see, butterflies and bees that conversed with one another and with the plants on which they fed, watched over by a parent council that guarded the interests of great and small, strong and weak, alike—the whole community presented a world of peace, goodwill, and happiness which no words of mine could convey a fair idea of.

"One thing I don't quite understand," said the Doctor to the vines, "is how you manage about seeding. Don't some of the plants throw down too much seed and bring forth a larger crop than is desirable?"

"That," said the whispering vines, "is taken care of by the birds. They have orders to eat up all the seed, except a certain quantity for each species of plant."

"Humph!" said the Doctor. "I hope I have not upset things for the council. I did a little experimental planting myself when I first arrived here. I had brought several kinds of seed with me from the earth, and I wanted to see how they would do in this climate. So far, however, the seeds have not come up at all."

The vines swayed slightly with a rustling sound that might easily have been a titter of amusement.

"You have forgotten, Doctor," said they, "that news travels fast in the moon. Your gardening experiments were seen and immediately reported to the council. And after you had gone back to your camp, every single seed that you had planted was carefully dug up by long-billed birds and destroyed. The council is awfully particular about seeds. It has to be. If we got overrun by any plant, weed, or shrub, all of our peaceful balance would be upset and goodness knows what might happen. Why, the president—"

The particular vines that were doing the talking were three large ones that hung close by the Doctor's shoulder. In a very sudden and curious manner they had broken off in the middle of what they were saying, like a person who had let something slip out in conversation that had been better left unsaid. Instantly, a tremendous excitement was visible throughout all the creepers that hung around the gulch. You never saw such swaying, writhing, twisting, and agitation. With squawks of alarm a number of brightly colored birds fluttered out of the curtain of leaves and flew away over the rocky shoulders above our heads.

"What's the matter? What has happened, Doctor?" I asked, as still more birds left the concealment of the creepers and disappeared in the distance.

"I've no idea, Stubbins," said he. "Someone has said a little too much, I fancy. Tell me," he asked, turning to the vines again: "Who is the president?"

"The president of the council," they replied after a pause.

"Every single seed was carefully dug up by long-billed birds"

"Yes, that I understand," said the Doctor. "But what, who, is he?"

For a little there was no answer, while the excitement and agitation broke out with renewed confusion among the long tendrils that draped the rocky alcove. Evidently some warnings and remarks were being exchanged that we were not to understand.

At last the original vines that had acted as spokesmen in the conversation addressed John Dolittle again.

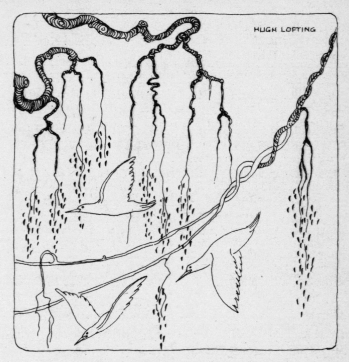

"Still more birds left the concealment of the creepers"

"We are sorry," they said, "but we have our orders. Certain things we have been forbidden to tell you."

"Who forbade you?" asked the Doctor.

But from then on, not a single word would they answer. The Doctor made several attempts to get them talking again but without success. Finally we were compelled to give it up and return to camp—which we reached very late.

"I think," said Polynesia, as the Doctor, Chee-Chee, and I set about preparing the vegetarian supper, "that we sort of upset society in the moon this afternoon. Gracious, I never saw such a land in my life! And I've seen a few. I suppose that by now every bumblebee and weed on the whole globe is talking about the whispering vines and the slip they made in mentioning the president. *President!* Shiver my timbers! You'd think he were St. Peter himself! What are they making such a mystery about, I'd like to know."

"We'll probably learn pretty soon now," said the Doctor, cutting into a huge melonlike fruit. "I have a feeling that they won't think it worthwhile to hold aloof from us much longer. I hope not, anyway."

"Me, too," said Chee-Chee. "Frankly, this secrecy is beginning to get under my skin. I'd like to feel assured that we are going to be given a passage back to Puddleby. For a while, anyway, I've had enough of adventure."

"Oh, well, don't worry," said the Doctor. "I still feel convinced that we'll be taken care of. Whoever it was that got us up here did so with some good intention. When I have done what it is that's wanted of me, arrangements will be made for putting us back on the earth, never fear."

"Humph!" grunted Polynesia, who was cracking nuts on a limb above our heads. "I hope you're right. I'm none too sure, myself . . . no, none too sure."

· The Nineteenth Chapter ·
THE MOON MAN

That night was, I think, the most disturbed one that we spent in the whole course of our stay on the moon. Not one of us slept soundly or continuously. For one thing, our growth had proceeded at an alarming and prodigious rate; and what bedding we had (we slept in that mild climate with the blankets under us instead of over us) had become absurdly short and insufficient for our new figures. Knees and elbows spilled over the sides and got dreadfully sore on the hard earth. But besides that discomfort, we were again conscious throughout the whole night of mysterious noises and presences. Every one of us seemed to be uneasy in his mind. I remember waking up one time and hearing the Doctor, Chee-Chee, and Polynesia all talking in their sleep at the same time.

Hollow-eyed and unrested we finally, at daybreak, crawled out of our various roosts and turned silently to the business of getting breakfast. That veteran campaigner Polynesia was the first to pull herself

"With a very serious look on her old face"

together. She came back from examining the ground
about the camp with a very serious look on her old
face.

"Well," said she, "if there's anyone in the moon who
hasn't been messing around our bunks while we
slept, I'd like to know who it is."

"Why?" asked the Doctor. "Anything unusual?"

"Come and see," said the parrot, and led the way
out into the clearing that surrounded our bunks and
baggage.

Well, we were accustomed to finding tracks around our home, but this that Polynesia showed us was certainly something quite out of the ordinary. For a belt of a hundred yards or more about our headquarters, the earth and sand and mud were a mass of footprints. Strange insect tracks, the marks of enormous birds, and—most evident of all—numberless prints of that gigantic human foot that we had seen before.

"Tut-tut!" said the Doctor peevishly. "They don't do us any harm, anyway. What does it matter if they come and look at us in our sleep? I'm not greatly interested, Polynesia. Let us take breakfast. A few extra tracks don't make much difference."

We sat down and started the meal.

But John Dolittle's prophecy that the animal kingdom would not delay much longer in getting in touch with us was surprisingly and suddenly fulfilled. I had a piece of yam smeared with honey halfway to my mouth when I became conscious of an enormous shadow soaring over me. I looked up and there was the giant moth who had brought us from Puddleby! I could hardly believe my eyes. With a graceful sweep of his gigantic wings he settled down beside me—a battleship beside a mouse—as though such exact and accurate landings were no more than a part of the ordinary day's work.

We had no time to remark on the moth's arrival before two or three more of the same kind suddenly swept up from nowhere, fanned the dust all over us with their giant wings, and settled down beside their brother.

Next, various birds appeared. Some species among

"Others were unbelievably large"

these we had already seen in the vines. But there were many we had not: enormous storks, geese, swans, and several others. Half of them seemed little bigger than their own kind on the earth. But others were unbelievably large and were colored and shaped somewhat differently—though you could nearly always tell to what family they belonged.

Again, more than one of us opened our mouths to say something and then closed them as some new and stranger arrival made its appearance and joined

the gathering. The bees were the next. I remembered
then seeing different kinds on the earth, though I had
never made a study of them. Here they all came
trooping, magnified into great terrible-looking mon-
sters out of a dream: the big black bumblebee, the
little yellow bumblebee, the common honeybee, the
bright green fast-flying slender bee. And with them
came all their cousins and relatives, though there
never seemed to be more than two or three speci-
mens of each kind.

I could see that poor Chee-Chee was simply scared
out of his wits. And little wonder! Insects of this size
gathering silently about one were surely enough to
appall the stoutest heart. Yet to me they were not entirely terrible. Perhaps I was merely taking my cue
from the Doctor, who was clearly more interested
than alarmed. But besides that, the manner of the
creatures did not appear unfriendly. Serious and or-
derly, they seemed to be gathering according to a set
plan; and I felt sure that very soon something was
going to happen that would explain it all.

And sure enough, a few moments later, when the
ground about our camp was literally one solid mass
of giant insects and birds, we heard a tread. Usually a
footfall in the open air makes little or no sound at all
—though it must not be forgotten that we had found
that sound of any kind traveled much more readily
on the moon than on the earth. But this was something quite peculiar. Actually, it shook the ground under us in a way that might have meant an earth-
quake. Yet somehow one *knew* it was a tread.

Chee-Chee ran to the Doctor and hid under his

coat. Polynesia never moved, just sat there on her tree branch, looking rather peeved and impatient but evidently interested. I followed the direction of her gaze with my own eyes for I knew that her instinct was always a good guide. I found that she was watching the woods that surrounded the clearing where we had established our camp. Her beady little eyes were fixed immovably on a V-shaped cleft in the horizon of trees away to my left.

It is curious how in those important moments I always seemed to keep an eye on old Polynesia. I don't mean to say that I did not follow the Doctor and stand ready to take his orders. But whenever anything unusual or puzzling like this came up, especially a case where animals were concerned, it was my impulse to keep an eye on the old parrot to see how she was taking it.

Now I saw her cocking her head on one side—in a quite characteristic pose—looking upward toward the cleft in the forest wall. She was muttering something beneath her breath (probably in Swedish, her favorite swearing language), but I could not make out more than a low, peevish murmur. Presently, watching with her, I thought I saw the trees sway. Then something large and round seemed to come in view above them in the cleft.

It was now growing dusk. It had taken, we suddenly realized, a whole day for the creatures to gather; and in our absorbed interest we had not missed our meals. One could not be certain of his vision. I noticed the Doctor suddenly half rise, spilling poor old Chee-Chee out upon the ground. The big round thing above the treetops grew bigger and higher. It swayed gently as it came forward and with it the forest swayed also, as grass moves when a cat stalks through it.

Any minute I was expecting the Doctor to say something. The creature approaching, whatever—whoever—it was, must clearly be so monstrous that everything we had met with on the moon so far would dwindle into insignificance in comparison.

And still old Polynesia sat motionless on her limb muttering and spluttering like a firecracker on a damp night.

Very soon we could hear other sounds from the oncoming creature besides his earth-shaking footfall. Giant trees snapped and crackled beneath his tread like twigs under a mortal's foot. I confess that an ominous terror clutched at my heart, too, now. I could sympathize with poor Chee-Chee's timidity. Oddly enough though, at this, the most terrifying moment in all our experience on the moon, the monkey did not try to conceal himself. He was standing beside the Doctor, fascinatedly watching the great shadow towering above the trees.

Onward, nearer, came the lumbering figure. Soon there was no mistaking its shape. It had cleared the woods now. The gathered insects and waiting birds were making way for it. Suddenly we realized that it was towering over us, quite near, its long arms hanging at its sides. *It was human.*

We had seen the Moon Man at last!

"Well, for pity's sake!" squawked Polynesia, breaking the awed silence. "You may be a frightfully

"It was human!"

important person here, but my goodness, it has taken you an awfully long time to come and call on us!"

Serious as the occasion was, in all conscience, Polynesia's remarks, continued in an uninterrupted stream of annoyed criticism, finally gave me the giggles. And after I once got started I couldn't have kept a straight face if I had been promised a fortune.

The dusk had now settled down over the strange assembly. Starlight glowed weirdly in the eyes of the moths and birds that stood about us, like a lamp's

" 'Look!—*the right wrist*—look!' "

flame reflected in the eyes of a cat. As I made another effort to stifle my silly titters I saw John Dolittle, the size of his figure looking perfectly absurd in comparison with the Moon Man's, rise to meet the giant who had come to visit us.

"I am glad to meet you—at last," said he in dignified well-bred English. A curious grunt of incomprehension was all that met his civility.

Then, seeing that the Moon Man evidently did not follow his language, John Dolittle set to work to find some tongue that would be understandable to him. I suppose there never was, and probably never will be, anyone who had the command of languages that the Doctor had. One by one he ran through most of the earthly human tongues that are used today or have been preserved from the past. None of them had the slightest effect upon the Moon Man. Turning to animal languages, however, the Doctor met with slightly better results. A word here and there seemed to be understood.

But it was when John Dolittle fell back on the languages of the insect and vegetable kingdoms that the Moon Man at last began to wake up and show interest. With fixed gaze, Chee-Chee, Polynesia, and I watched the two figures as they wrestled with the problems of common speech. Minute after minute went by, hour after hour. Finally the Doctor made a signal to me behind his back, and I knew that now he was really ready. I picked up my notebook and pencil from the ground.

As I laid back a page in preparation for dictation, there came a strange cry from Chee-Chee:

"Look! *The right wrist!* Look!"

We peered through the twilight . . . Yes, there *was* something around the giant's wrist, but so tight that it was almost buried in the flesh. The Doctor touched it gently. But before he could say anything Chee-Chee's voice broke out again, his words cutting the stillness in a curious hoarse, sharp whisper.

"*The blue stone beads!* Don't you see them? . . . They don't fit him anymore since he's grown into a giant. But he's Otho Bludge, the artist. That's the bracelet he got from Pippiteepa, the grandmother of the fairies! It is he, Doctor, Otho Bludge, who was blown off the earth in the *days before there was a moon*!"

· The Twentieth Chapter ·
THE DOCTOR AND THE GIANT

All right, Chee-Chee, all right," said the Doctor hurriedly. "Wait now. We'll see what we can find out. Don't get excited."

In spite of the Doctor's reassuring words I could see that he himself was by this time quite a little agitated. And for that no one could blame him. After weeks in this weird world where naught but extraordinary things came up day after day, we had been constantly wondering when we'd see the strange human whose traces and influence were everywhere so evident. Now at last he had appeared.

I gazed up at the gigantic figure rearing away into the skies above our heads. With one of his feet he could easily have crushed the lot of us like so many cockroaches. Yet he, with the rest of the gathering, seemed not unfriendly to us, if a bit puzzled by our size. As for John Dolittle, he may have been a little upset by Chee-Chee's announcement, but he certainly wasn't scared. He at once set to work to get into touch with this strange creature who had called on us. And, as was usual with his experiments of this kind, the other side seemed more than willing to help.

The giant wore very few clothes. A garment somewhat similar to our own, made from the flexible bark and leaves we had discovered in the forest, covered his middle from the armpits down to the lower thighs. His hair was long and shaggy, falling almost to his shoulders. The Doctor measured up to a line somewhere near his anklebone. Apparently realizing that it was difficult for John Dolittle to talk with him at that range, the giant made a movement with his hand and at once the insects nearest to us rose and crawled away. In the space thus cleared the manmonster sat down to converse with his visitors from the earth.

It was curious that after this I, too, no longer feared the enormous creature who looked like something from a fairy tale or a nightmare. Stretching down a tremendous hand, he lifted the Doctor, as though he had been a doll, and set him upon his bare knee. From this height—at least thirty feet above my head—John Dolittle clambered still farther up the giant's frame till he stood upon his shoulder.

Here he apparently had much greater success in making himself understood than he had had lower down. By standing on tiptoe he could just reach the Moon Man's ear. Presently descending to the knee again, he began calling to *me*.

"Stubbins!—I say, Stubbins! Have you got a notebook handy?"

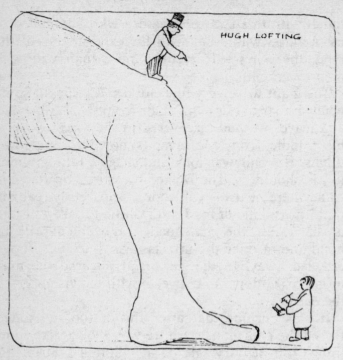

HUGH LOFTING

" 'Stubbins!—I say, Stubbins!' "

"Yes, Doctor. In my pocket. Do you want me to take dictation?"

"Please," he shouted back—for all the world like a foreman yelling orders from a high building. "Get this down. I have hardly established communication yet, but I want you to take some preliminary notes. Are you ready?"

As a matter of fact, the Doctor in his enthusiasm had misjudged how easy he'd find it to converse with the Moon Man. For a good hour I stood waiting with my pencil poised, and no words for dictation were handed down. Finally, the Doctor called to me that he would have to delay matters a little till he got in close touch with our giant visitor.

"Humph!" grunted Polynesia. "I don't see why he bothers. I never saw such an unattractive enormous brute. Doesn't look as though he had the wits of a caterpillar, anyway. And to think that it was this great lump of unintelligent mutton that has kept the Doctor—John Dolittle, M.D.—and the rest of us, hanging about till it suited him to call on us! After sending for us, mind you! That's the part that rattles me!"

"Oh, but goodness!" muttered Chee-Chee, peering up at the towering figure in the dusk. "Think—*think* how old he is! That man was living when the moon separated from the earth—thousands, maybe millions, of years ago! Golly, what an age!"

"Yes, he's old enough to know better," snapped the parrot, "—better manners anyway. Just because he's fat and overgrown is no reason why he should treat his guests with such outrageous rudeness."

"Oh, but come now, Polynesia," I said, "we must not forget that this is a human being who has been separated from his own kind for centuries and centuries. And even such civilization as he knew on the earth, way back in those Stone-Age days, was not, I imagine, anything to boast of. Pretty crude, I'll bet it was, the world then. The wonder is, to my way of thinking, that he has any mind at all—with no other humans to mingle with through all that countless

time. I'm not surprised that John Dolittle finds it difficult to talk with him."

"Oh, well, now, Tommy Stubbins," said she, "that
may sound all very scientific and highfalutin. But just
the same, there's no denying that this overgrown
booby was the one who got us up here. And the least
he could have done was to see that we were properly
received and cared for—instead of letting us fish for
ourselves with no one to guide us or to put us on to
the ropes. Very poor hospitality, I call it."

"You seem to forget, Polynesia," I said mildly, "that
in spite of our small size, we may have seemed—as
the Doctor said—quite as fearful to him and his
world as he and his have been to us—even if he did
arrange to get us here. Did you notice that he
limped?"

"I did," said she, tossing her head. "He dragged his
left foot after him with an odd gait. Pshaw! I'll bet
that's what he got the Doctor up here for—rheumatism or a splinter in his toe. Still, what I *don't* understand is how he heard of John Dolittle, famous
though he is, with no communication between his
world and ours."

It was very interesting to me to watch the Doctor
trying to talk with the Moon Man. I could not make
the wildest guess at what sort of language it could be
that they would finally hit upon. After all that time of
separation from his fellows, how much could this
strange creature remember of a mother tongue?

As a matter of fact, I did not find out that evening
at all. The Doctor kept at his experiments, in his
usual way, entirely forgetful of time or anything else.

" 'Very poor hospitality, I call it' "

After I had watched for a while Chee-Chee's head nodding sleepily, I finally dozed off myself.

When I awoke it was daylight. The Doctor was still engaged with the giant in his struggles to understand and be understood. However, I could see at once that he was encouraged. I shouted up to him that it was breakfast time. He heard, nodded back to me, and then apparently asked the giant to join us at our meal. I was surprised and delighted to see with what ease he managed to convey this idea to our big

HUGH LOFTING

"I watched Chee-Chee's head nodding sleepily"

friend. For the Moon Man at once sat him down upon
the ground near our tarpaulin, which served as a ta-
blecloth, and gazed critically over the foodstuffs laid
out. We offered him some of our famous yellow yam.
At this he shook his head vigorously. Then with signs
and grunts he proceeded to explain something to
John Dolittle.

"He tells me, Stubbins," said the Doctor presently,
"that the yellow yam is the principal cause of rapid
growth. Everything in this world, it seems, tends to-

ward size; but this particular food is the worst. He advises us to drop it—unless we want to grow as big as he is. He has been trying to get back to our size, apparently, for ever so long."

"Try him with some of the melon, Doctor," said Chee-Chee.

This, when offered to the Moon Man, was accepted gladly; and for a little we all munched in silence.

"How are you getting on with his language, Doctor?" I asked presently.

"Oh, so-so," he grumbled. "It's odd—awfully strange. At first I supposed it would be something like most human languages, a variation of vocal sounds. And I tried for hours to get in touch with him along those lines. But it was only a few vague far-off memories that I could bring out. I was, of course, particularly interested to link up a connection with some earthly language. Finally I went on to the languages of the insects and the plants and found that he spoke all dialects, in both, perfectly. On the whole I am awfully pleased with my experiments. Even if I cannot link him up with some of our own dead languages, at least his superior knowledge of the insect and vegetable tongues will be of great value to me."

"Has he said anything so far about why he got you up here?" asked Polynesia.

"Not as yet," said the Doctor. "But we've only just begun, you know. All in good time, Polynesia, all in good time."

· The Twenty-first Chapter ·

HOW OTHO BLUDGE
CAME TO THE MOON

The Doctor's warning to the parrot that perhaps we were just as terrifying to the Moon Man (in spite of his size) as he and his world were to us, proved to be quite true. After breakfast was over and I got out the usual notebook for dictation it soon appeared that this giant, the dread president of the council, was the mildest creature living. He let us crawl all over him and seemed quite pleased that we took so much interest in him. This did not appear to surprise the Doctor, who from the start had regarded him as a friend. But to Chee-Chee and myself, who had thought that he might gobble us up at any moment, it was, to say the least, a great relief.

I will not set down here in detail that first talk between the Moon Man and the Doctor. It was very long and went into a great many matters of languages and natural history that might not be of great interest to the general reader. But here and there in my report of that conversation I may dictate it word for word, where such a course may seem necessary to give a clear picture of the ideas exchanged. For it was certainly an interview of great importance.

The Doctor began by questioning the giant on the history that Chee-Chee had told us as it had been handed down to him by his grandmother. Here the Moon Man's memory seemed very vague; but when prompted with details from the monkeys' history, he occasionally responded and more than once agreed with the Doctor's statements or corrected them with a good deal of certainty and firmness.

I think I ought perhaps to say something here about the Moon Man's face. In the pale daylight of a lunar dawn it looked clever and intelligent enough, but not nearly so old as one would have expected. It is indeed hard to describe that face. It wasn't brutish and yet it had in it something quite foreign to the average human countenance as seen on the earth. I imagine that his being separated from humankind for so long may have accounted for this. Beyond question it was an animallike countenance and yet it was entirely free from anything like ferocity. If one could imagine a kindly animal who had used all his faculties in the furtherance of helpful and charitable ends, one would have the nearest possible idea of the face of the Moon Man, as I saw it clearly for the first time when he took breakfast with us that morning.

In the strange tongues of insects and plants John Dolittle fired off question after question at our giant guest. Yes, he admitted, he probably was Otho Bludge, the prehistoric artist. This bracelet? Yes, he wore it because someone . . . And then his memory failed him . . . What someone? . . . Well, anyway, he remembered that it had first been worn by a woman before he had it. What matter, after all? It was long ago, terribly long. Was there anything else that we would like to know?

There was a question I myself wanted to ask. The night before, in my wanderings with Chee-Chee over the giant's huge body, I had discovered a disc or plate hanging to his belt. In the dusk then I had not been able to make out what it was. But this morning I got a better view of it: the most exquisite picture of a girl kneeling with a bow and arrow in her hands, carved upon a plate of reindeer horn. I asked the Doctor if he didn't want to question the Moon Man about it. We all guessed, of course, from Chee-Chee's story, what it was. But I thought it might prompt the giant's memory to things out of the past that would be of value to the Doctor. I even whispered to John Dolittle that the giant might be persuaded to give it to us or barter it for something. Even I knew enough about museum relics to realize its tremendous value.

The Doctor indeed did speak of it to him. The giant raised it from his belt, where it hung by a slender thong of bark and gazed at it a while. A spark of recollection lit up his eyes for a moment. Then, with a pathetic fumbling sort of gesture, he pressed it to his heart a moment while that odd fuddled look came over his countenance once more. The Doctor and I, I think, both felt we had been rather tactless and did not touch upon the subject again.

I have often been since—though I certainly was not at the time—amused at the way the Doctor took charge of the situation and raced all over this enormous creature as though he were some new kind of specimen to be labeled and docketed for a naturalhistory museum. Yet he did it in such a way as not to give the slightest offense.

"Yes. Very good," said he. "We have now established you as Otho Bludge, the Stone-Age artist, who was blown off the earth when the moon set herself up in the sky. But how about this council? I understand you are president of it and can control its workings. Is that so?"

The great giant swung his enormous head around and regarded for a moment the pigmy figure of the Doctor standing, just then, on his forearm.

"The council?" said he dreamily. "Oh, ah, yes, to be sure, the council . . . Well, we had to establish that, you know. At one time it was nothing but war—war, war all the time. We saw that if we did not arrange a balance we would have an awful mess. Too many seeds. Plants spread like everything. Birds laid too many eggs. Bees swarmed too often. Terrible! You've seen that down there on the earth, I imagine, have you not?"

"Yes, yes, to be sure," said the Doctor. "Go on, please."

"Well, there isn't much more to that. We just made sure, by means of the council, that there should be *no more warfare.*"

"Humph!" the Doctor grunted. "But tell me, how is it you yourself have lived so long? No one knows how many years ago it is that the moon broke away from the earth. And your age, compared with the life of Man in our world, must be something staggering."

"Well, of course," said the Moon Man, "just how I got here is something that I have never been able to explain completely, even to myself. But why bother? Here I am. What recollections I have of that time are awfully hazy. Let me see, when I came to myself I could hardly breathe. I remember that. The air—everything—was so different. But I was determined to survive. That, I think, is what must have saved me. I was *determined* to survive. This piece of land, I recollect, when it stopped swirling was pretty barren. But it had the remnants of trees and plants that it had brought with it from the earth. I lived on roots and all manner of stuff to begin with. Many a time I thought that I would have to perish. But I didn't— *because I was determined to survive.* And in the end I did. After a while plants began to grow; insects, which had come with the plants, flourished. Birds the same way—they, like me, were determined to survive. A new world was formed. Years after, I realized that I was the one to steer and guide its destiny, since I had—at that time anyway—more intelligence than the other forms of life. I saw what this fighting of kind against kind must lead to. So I formed the council. Since then—oh, dear, how long ago!—vegetable and animal species have come to— Well, you see it here . . . That's all. It's quite simple."

"Yes, yes," said the Doctor hurriedly. "I quite understand that—the necessities that led you to establish the council. And an exceedingly fine thing it is, in my opinion. We will come back to that later. In the

HUGH LOFTING

"I lived on roots"

meantime, I am greatly puzzled as to how you came to hear of me—with no communication between your world and ours. Your moth came to Puddleby and asked me to accompany him back here. It was you who sent him, I presume?"

"Well, it was I and the council who sent him," the Moon Man corrected. "As for the ways in which your reputation reached us, communication is, as you say, very rare between the two worlds. But it does occur once in a long while. Some disturbance takes place in your globe that throws particles so high that they get beyond the influence of earth gravity and come under the influence of our gravity. Then they are drawn to the moon and stay here. I remember, many centuries ago, a great whirlwind or some other form of rumpus in your world occurred that tossed shrubs and stones to such a height that they lost touch with the earth altogether and finally landed here. And a great nuisance they were, too. The shrubs seeded and spread like wildfire before we realized they had arrived, and we had a terrible time getting them under control."

"That is most interesting," said the Doctor, glancing in my direction, as he translated, to make sure I got the notes down in my book. "But please tell me of the occasion by which you first learned of me and decided you wanted me up here."

"That," said the Moon Man, "came about through something that was, I imagine, a volcanic eruption. From what I can make out, one of your big mountains down there suddenly blew its head off, after remaining quiet and peaceful for many years. It was an enormous and terribly powerful explosion, and tons of earth and trees and stuff were fired off into space. Some of this material that started away in the direction of the moon finally came within the influence of our attraction and was drawn to us. And, as you doubtless know, when earth or plants are shot away some animal life nearly always goes with it. In this case a bird, a kingfisher, in fact, who was building her nest in the banks of a mountain lake, was carried off. Several pieces of the earth landed on the moon.

HUGH LOFTING

"The piece fell into one of our lakes"

Some, striking land, were smashed to dust and any animal life they carried—mostly insect, of course—was destroyed. But the piece on which the kingfisher traveled fell into one of our lakes."

It was an astounding story and yet I believe it true. For how else could the Doctor's fame have reached the moon? Of course any but a water bird would have been drowned because apparently the mass plunged down fifty feet below the surface, but the kingfisher at once came up and flew off for the shore. It was a marvel that she was alive. I imagine her trip through the dead belt had been made at such tremendous speed that she managed to escape suffocation without the artificial breathing devices that we had been compelled to use.

· The Twenty-second Chapter ·

HOW THE MOON FOLK
HEARD OF DOCTOR DOLITTLE

The bird the Moon Man had spoken of (it seems she had since been elected to the council) was presently brought forward and introduced to the Doctor. She gave us some valuable information about her trip to the moon and how she had since adapted herself to new conditions.

She admitted it was she who had told the moon folk about John Dolittle and his wonderful skill in treating sicknesses, of his great reputation among the birds, beasts, and fishes of the earth.

It was through this introduction also that we learned that the gathering about us was nothing less than a full assembly of the council itself—with the exception, of course, of the vegetable kingdom, who could not come. That community was, however, represented by different creatures from the insect and bird worlds, who were there to see to it that its interests were properly looked after.

This was evidently a big day for the moon people.

"The bird was introduced to the Doctor"

After our interview with the kingfisher we could see that arguments were going on between different groups and parties all over the place. At times it looked like a political meeting of the rowdiest kind. These discussions the Doctor finally put down quite firmly by demanding of the Moon Man in a loud voice the reason for his being summoned here.

"After all," said he, when some measure of quiet had been restored, "you must realize that I am a very busy man. I appreciate it as a great honor that I have been asked to come here. But I have duties and obligations to perform on the earth, which I have left. I presume that you asked me here for some special purpose. Won't you please let me know what it is?"

A silent pause spread over the chattering assembly. I glanced around the queer audience of birds and bugs who squatted, listening. The Doctor, quite apart from his demand for attention, had evidently touched upon a ticklish subject. Even the Moon Man himself seemed somewhat ill at ease.

"Well," he said at last, "the truth is we were sorely in need of a good physician. I myself have been plagued by a bad pain in the foot. And then many of the bigger insects—the grasshoppers especially— have been in very poor health now for some time. From what the kingfisher told me, I felt you were the only one who could help us . . . that you—er—perhaps wouldn't mind if we got you up here where your skill was so sorely needed. Tell me now, you were not put out by the confidence we placed in you? We had no one in our own world who could help us. Therefore we agreed, in a special meeting of the council, to send down and try to get you."

The Doctor made no reply.

"You must realize," the Moon Man went on, his voice dropping to a still more apologetic tone, "that this moth we sent took his life in his hand. We cast lots among the larger birds, moths, butterflies, and other insects. It had to be one of our larger kinds. It was a long trip, requiring enormous staying power . . ."

The Moon Man spread out his giant hands in

protest—a gesture very suggestive of the other world from which he originally came. The Doctor hastened to reassure him.

"Why, of course, of course," said he. "I—we—were most glad to come. In spite of the fact that I am always terribly busy down there, this was something so new and promising in natural history I laid every interest aside in my eagerness to get here. With the moth you sent, the difficulty of language did not permit me to make the preparations I would have liked. But, pray, do not think that I have regretted coming. I would not have missed this experience for worlds. It is true I could have wished that you had seen your way to getting in touch with us sooner. But there—I imagine you, too, have your difficulties. I suppose you must be kept pretty busy."

"Busy?" said the Moon Man blankly. "Oh, no. I'm not busy. Life is very quiet and pleasant here—sometimes too quiet, we think. A session with the council every now and then and a general inspection of the globe every so often: that is all I have to bother with. The reason I didn't come and see you sooner, to be quite honest, was because I was a bit scared. It was something so new, having human folks visit you from another world. There was no telling what you might turn out to be—what you might do. For another thing, I expected you to be alone. For weeks past I have had the birds and insects—and the plants, too—send me reports of your movements and character. You see, I had relied solely on the statements of a kingfisher. No matter how kind and helpful you had been to the creatures of your own world, it did

HUGH LOFTING

"I had the birds bring me reports of your movements"

not follow that you would be the same way inclined toward the moon folk. I am sorry if I did not appear properly hospitable. But you must make allowances. It—it was all so—so new."

"Oh, quite, quite," said the Doctor, again most anxious to make his host feel at ease. "Say no more, please, of that. I understand perfectly. There are a few points, however, on which I would like to have some light thrown. For one thing, we thought we saw smoke on the moon, from Puddleby, shortly after your moth arrived. Can you tell us anything about that?"

"Why, of course," said the Moon Man quickly. "I did that. We were quite worried about the moth. As I told you, we felt kind of guilty about the risky job we had given him. It was Jamaro who finally drew the marked card in the lottery."

"Jamaro!" muttered the Doctor, slightly bewildered. "Lottery? I—er—"

"The lottery to decide who should go," the Moon Man explained. "I told you: We drew lots. Jamaro Bumblelily was the moth who drew the ticket that gave the task to him."

"Oh, I see," said the Doctor. "Jamaro. Yes, yes. You give your insects names in this land. Very natural and proper, of course, where they are so large and take such an important part in the life and government of the community. You can no doubt tell all these insects one from another, even when they belong to the same species?"

"Certainly," said the Moon Man. "We have, I suppose, several hundreds of thousands of bees in the moon. But I know each one by his first name, as well as his swarm, or family, name. Anyhow, to continue: It was then Jamaro Bumblelily who drew the ticket that gave him the job of going to the earth after you. He was very sportsmanlike and never grumbled a bit. But we were naturally anxious. It is true that creatures had come, at rare intervals, from the earth to our world. But so far none had gone from us to the earth. We had only the vaguest idea of what your world would be like—from the descriptions of the kingfisher. And even in getting those we had been greatly handicapped by language. It had only been after days and weeks of work that we had been able to understand one another in the roughest way. So we had arranged with Jamaro Bumblelily that as soon as he landed he was to try and find some way to signal us to let us know he was all right. And we were to signal back to him. It seems he made a bad landing and lay helpless in your garden for some days. For a long while we waited in great anxiety. We feared he must have perished in his heroic exploit. Then we thought that maybe if we signaled to him he would be encouraged and know that we were still expecting his return. So we set off the smoke smudge."

"Yes," said the Doctor. "I saw it, even if Jamaro didn't. But tell me, how did you manage to raise such an enormous smudge? It must have been as big as a mountain."

"True," said the Moon Man. "For twenty days before Jamaro's departure I and most of the larger birds and insects had gathered the jing-jing bark from the forest."

"Gathered the *what?*" asked the Doctor.

"The jing-jing bark," the Moon Man repeated. "It is a highly explosive bark from a certain tree we have here."

"But how did you light it?" asked the Doctor.

"By friction," said the Moon Man, "—drilling a hardwood stick into a softwood log. We had tons and tons of the bark piled in a barren rocky valley where it would be safe from firing the bush or jungle. We are always terrified of bushfires here—our world is

"I set the pile off with a live ember"

not large, you know. I set the pile off with a live ember that I carried on a slate. Then I sprang back behind a rock bluff to defend my eyes. The explosion was terrific, and the smoke kept us all coughing for days before it finally cleared away."

· The Twenty-third Chapter ·

THE MAN WHO
MADE HIMSELF A KING

We were frequently reminded during this long conversation (it lasted over a full day and a half) that the strange crowd about us was the great council itself. Questions every now and then were hurled at the Moon Man from the dimness of the rear. He was continually turning his head as messages and inquiries were carried across to him from mouth to mouth. Sometimes without consulting the Doctor further he would answer them himself in queer sounds and signs. It was quite evident that the council was determined to keep in touch with any negotiations that were going on.

As for John Dolittle, there was so much that he wanted to find out, it looked—in spite of his hurry to get back to the earth—as though his queries would never end, which, in a first meeting between two worlds, is not after all to be wondered at.

"Can you remember," he asked, "when you first felt the moon steadying herself, how you got accustomed

to the new conditions? We had on our arrival a perfectly terrible time, you know. Different air, different
gravity, different hearing, and the rest. Tell me, how
did you manage?"

Frowning, the Moon Man passed his gigantic hand
across his brow.

"Really—it's so long ago," he muttered. "As I told
you, I nearly died many times. Getting enough food
to stay alive on kept me busy the first few months.
Then when I was sure that that problem was solved, I
began to watch. Soon I saw that the birds and insects
were faced with the same difficulties as I was. I
searched the moon globe from end to end. There
were no others of my own kind here. I was the only
man. I needed company badly. 'All right,' I said, 'I'll
study the insect and bird kingdoms.' The birds
adapted themselves much quicker than I did to the
new conditions. I soon found that they, being in the
same boat as myself, were only too glad to cooperate
with me in anything that would contribute to our
common good. Of course, I was careful to kill nothing. For one thing I had no desire to; and for another
I realized that if, on such a little globe, I started to
make enemies, I could not last long. From the beginning I had done my best to live and let live. With no
other human to talk with I can't tell you how terribly,
desperately lonely I felt. Then I decided I'd try to
learn the language of the birds. Clearly, they had a
language. No one could listen to their warblings and
not see that. For years I worked at it—often terribly
discouraged at my poor progress. Finally—don't ask
me when—I got to the point where I could whistle

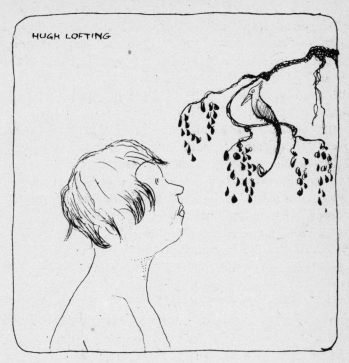

HUGH LOFTING

"I could whistle short conversations"

short conversations with them. Then came the insects —the birds helped me in that, too. Then the plant languages. The bees started me. They knew all the dialects. And . . . well . . ."

"Go on," said the Doctor. The tone of his voice was calm and quiet, but I could see that he was deeply, intensely interested.

"Oh, dear me," sighed the Moon Man, almost petulantly, "my memory, you know, for dates as far back as that, is awfully poor. Today it seems as though I had talked Heron and Geranium all my life. But just when it was, actually, that I reached the point where I could converse freely with the insects and plants, I couldn't give you the vaguest idea. I do know that it took me far, far longer to get in touch with the vegetable forms of life than it did with either the insects or the birds. I am afraid that our keeping count of time throughout has been pretty sketchy—certainly in our earlier history, anyway. But then you must remember we were occupied with a great number of far more serious tasks. Recently—the last thousand years or so—we have been making an effort to keep a history and we can show you, I think, a pretty good record of most of the more important events within that time. The trouble is that nearly all of the dates you want are earlier than that."

"Well, never mind," said the Doctor. "We are getting on very well under the circumstances. I would like very much to see that record you speak of and will ask you to show it to me, if you will be so good, later."

He then entered into a long examination of the Moon Man (carefully avoiding all dates, periods, and references to time) on a whole host of subjects. The majority of them were concerned with insect and plant evolution, and he kept a strict eye on me to see that all questions and replies were jotted down in the notebook. Gracious! What an unending list it seemed to my tired mind! How had the Moon Man first realized that the plants were anxious to talk and cooperate with him? What had led him to believe that the bees were in communication with the flowers they fed on? Which fruits and vegetables had he found were good for human food and how had he discovered their nutritious qualities without poisoning himself? Etc., etc., etc. It went on for hours. I got most of it down, with very few mistakes, I think. But I know I was more than half asleep during the last hours of the interview.

The only trouble with most of it was this same old bugbear of time. After all these ages of living without human company, the poor giant's mind had gotten to the point where it simply didn't *use* time. Even in this record of the last thousand years, which he had proudly told us was properly dated, we found, when he showed it to us, an error of a century more or less meant very little.

This history had been carved in pictures and signs on the face of a wide, flat rock. The workmanship of Otho the prehistoric artist showed up here to great advantage. While the carvings were not by any means to be compared with his masterpiece of the kneeling girl, they nevertheless had a dash and beauty of design that would arrest the attention of almost anyone.

Nevertheless, despite the errors of time, both in his recollections and his graven history, we got down the best record that we could in the circumstances. And with all its slips and gaps it was a most thrilling and exciting document. It was the story of a new world's evolution; of how a man, suddenly transported into space with nothing but what his two hands held at the moment of the catastrophe, had made himself the kindly monarch of a kingdom—a kingdom more

"This history had been carved in pictures
on the face of a rock"

wondrous than the wildest imaginings of the mortals
he had left behind. For he was indeed a king, even if
he called himself no more than the president of the
council. And what hardships and terrible difficulties
he had overcome in doing it, only we could realize—
we, who had come here with advantages and aids
that he had never known.

Finally a lull did come in this long, long conversation between the Doctor and the Moon Man. And

while I lay back and stretched my right hand, cramped from constant writing, Polynesia gave vent to a great deal that she had evidently had on her mind for some time.

"Well," she grunted, lifting her eyebrows, "what did I tell you, Tommy? Rheumatism! That's what the Doctor has come all this way for—*rheumatism!* I wouldn't mind it so much in the case of the Moon Man himself. Because he certainly is a man in a hundred. But *grasshoppers!* Think of it! Think of bringing John Dolittle, M.D., billions of miles" (Polynesia's ideas on geographical measurement were a bit sketchy) "just to wait on a bunch of grasshoppers! I—"

But the remainder of her indignant speech got mixed up with some of her favorite Swedish swear words, and the result was something that no one could make head or tail of.

Very soon this pause in the conversation between the Doctor and the Moon Man was filled up by a great deal of talking among the council. Every member of that important parliament apparently wanted to know exactly what had been said and decided on and what new measures—if any—were to be put in force. We could see that the poor president was being kept very busy.

At length, the Doctor turned once more to the giant and said, "Well, now, when would it be convenient for you and the insect patients to be examined? I shall be most happy to do everything possible for you all, but you must realize that I would like to get back to the earth as soon as I conveniently can."

" 'But *grasshoppers!*' "

Before answering, the Moon Man proceeded to consult his council behind him. And, to judge from the length of the discussions that followed, he was meeting with quite a little criticism in whatever plans he was proposing. But finally he managed to quiet them; and addressing John Dolittle once more, he said, "Thank you. If it will not inconvenience you, we will come tomorrow and have you minister to us. You have been very kind to come at all. I hope we will not seem too large an undertaking for you. At least, since you have approved of our system and government here, you will have the satisfaction of knowing that you are assisting us in a time of great need."

"Why, of course, of course," said the Doctor at once. "I shall be only too glad. That is what I am for, after all. I am a doctor, you know, a physician—even if I have become a naturalist in my later years. At what hour will you be ready for me?"

"At dawn," said the Moon Man. Even in these modern days, ideas of time on the moon seemed strangely simple. "We will wait on you at sunrise. Till then, pleasant dreams and good rest!"

· The Twenty-fourth Chapter ·

DOCTOR DOLITTLE OPENS
HIS SURGERY ON THE MOON

Even the garrulous Polynesia was too tired to talk much more that night. For all of us it had been a long and steady session, that interview, tense with excitement. The Moon Man and his council had barely departed before every one of us was dozing off without a change of clothes or a bite to eat. I am sure that nothing on earth—or moon—could have disturbed our slumbers.

The daylight was just beginning to show when we were awakened. I am not certain who was the first to arouse himself (probably John Dolittle), but I do know that I was the first to get up.

What a strange sight! In the dim light hundreds, perhaps thousands, of gigantic insects, all invalids, stood about our camp, staring at the tiny human physician who had come so far to cure their ailments. Some of these creatures we had not so far seen and never even suspected their presence on the moon: caterpillars as long as a village street, with gout in a dozen feet; immense beetles suffering from an afflic-

HUGH LOFTING

"Grasshoppers with crude bandages on their gawky joints"

tion of the eyes; grasshoppers as tall as a three-story house, with crude bandages on their gawky joints; enormous birds with a wing held painfully in an odd position. The Doctor's home had become once more a clinic, and all the halt and lame of moon society had gathered at his door.

The great man, when I finally roused him, swallowed two or three gulps of melon, washed them down with a draft of honey and water, took off his coat, and set to work.

Of course, the poor little black bag, which had done such yeoman service for many years in many lands, was not equal to a demand like this. The first thing to run out was the supply of bandages. Chee-Chee and I tore up blankets and shirts to make more. Then the embrocation became exhausted; next the iodine and the rest of the antiseptics. But in his botanical studies of the trees and plants of this world, the Doctor had observed and experimented with several things that he had found helpful in rheumatic conditions and other medical uses. Chee-Chee and Polynesia were dispatched at once to find the herbs and roots and leaves that he wanted.

For hours and hours he worked like a slave. It seemed as though the end of the line of patients would never be reached. But finally he did get the last of them fixed up and dispatched. It was only then he realized that the Moon Man had let all the other sufferers come forward ahead of himself. Dusk was coming on. The Doctor peered around the great space about our camp. It was empty, save for a giant figure that squatted silent, motionless, and alone, by the forest's edge.

"My goodness!" muttered the Doctor. "I had entirely forgotten him. And he never uttered a word. Well, no one can say he is selfish. That, I fancy, is why he rules here. I must see what is the matter with him at once."

John Dolittle hurried across the open space and questioned the giant. An enormous left leg was stretched out for his examination. Like a fly, the

HUGH LOFTING

"Then he lectured his big friend"

Doctor traveled rapidly up and down it, pinching and squeezing and testing here and there.

"More gout," he said at last with definite decision. "A bad enough case, too. Now listen, Otho Bludge."

Then he lectured his big friend for a long time. Mostly it seemed about diet but there was a great deal concerning anatomy, exercise, dropsy, and *starch* in it, too.

At the end of it the Moon Man seemed quite a little impressed, much happier in his mind, and a great deal more lively and hopeful. Finally, after thanking the Doctor at great length, he departed, while the ground shook again beneath his limping tread.

Once more we were all fagged out and desperately sleepy.

"Well," said the Doctor as he arranged his one remaining blanket on his bed, "I think that's about all we can do. Tomorrow—or maybe the next day—we will, if all goes well, start back for Puddleby."

"*Sh!*" whispered Polynesia. "There's someone listening. I'm sure—over there behind those trees."

"Oh, pshaw!" said the Doctor. "No one could hear us at that range."

"Don't forget how sound travels on the moon," warned the parrot.

"But, my goodness!" said the Doctor. "They *know* we've got to go sometime. We can't stay here forever. Didn't I tell the president himself I had jobs to attend to on the earth? If I felt they needed me badly enough I wouldn't mind staying quite a while yet. But there's Stubbins, here. He came away without even telling his parents where he was going or how long it might be before he returned. I don't know what Jacob Stubbins may be thinking, or his good wife. Probably worried to death. I—"

"Sh! *Sh!* Will you be quiet?" whispered Polynesia again. "Didn't you hear that? I tell you there's some-one listening—or I'm a double Dutchman. Pipe down, for pity's sake. There are ears all around us. Go to sleep!"

We all took the old parrot's advice—only too willingly. And very soon every one of us was snoring.

This time we did not awaken early. We had no jobs to attend to, and we took advantage of a chance to snooze away as long as we wished.

It was nearly midday again when we finally got stirring. We were in need of water for breakfast. Getting the water had always been Chee-Chee's job. This morning, however, the Doctor wanted him to hunt up a further supply of medicinal plants for his surgical work. I volunteered therefore to act as water carrier.

With several vessels that we had made from gourds I started out for the forests.

I had once or twice performed this same office of emergency water carrier before. I was therefore able, on reaching the edge of the jungle, to make straight for the place where we usually got our supplies.

I hadn't gone very far before Polynesia overtook me.

"Watch out, Tommy!" said she in a mysterious whisper as she settled on my shoulder.

"Why?" I asked. "Is anything amiss?"

"I don't quite know," said she. "But I'm uneasy and I wanted to warn you. Listen, that whole crowd that came to be doctored yesterday, you know? Well, not one of them has shown up again since. Why?"

There was a pause.

"Well," said I presently, "I don't see any particular reason why they should. They got their medicine, their treatment. Why should they pester the Doctor further? It's a jolly good thing that some patients leave him alone after they are treated, isn't it?"

"True, true," said she. "Just the same, their all staying away the next day looks fishy to me. They didn't

" 'Watch out, Tommy!' "

all get treated. There's something in it. I feel it in my bones. And besides, I can't find the Moon Man himself. I've been hunting everywhere for him. He, too, has gone into hiding again, just the same as they all did when we first arrived here . . . Well, look out! That's all. I must go back now. But keep your eyes open, Tommy. Good luck!"

I couldn't make head or tail of the parrot's warning and, greatly puzzled, I proceeded on my way to the pool to fill my waterpots.

There I found the Moon Man. It was a strange and sudden meeting. I had no warning of his presence till I was actually standing in the water filling the gourds. Then a movement of one of his feet revealed his immense form squatting in the concealment of the dense jungle. He rose to his feet as soon as he saw that I perceived him.

His expression was not unfriendly—just as usual, a kindly, calm half smile. Yet I felt at once uneasy and a little terrified. Lame as he was, his speed and size made escape by running out of the question. He did not understand my language, nor I his. It was a lonely spot, deep in the woods. No cry for help would be likely to reach the Doctor's ears.

I was not left long in doubt as to his intentions. Stretching out his immense right hand, he lifted me out of the water as though I were a specimen of some flower he wanted for a collection. Then, with enormous strides, he carried me away through the forest. One step of his was half an hour's journey for me. And yet it seemed as though he put his feet down very softly, presumably in order that his usual thunderous tread should not be heard—or felt—by others.

At length he stopped. He had reached a wide clearing. Jamaro Bumblelily, the same moth that had brought us from the earth, was waiting. The Moon Man set me down upon the giant insect's back. I heard the low rumble of his voice as he gave some final orders. I had been kidnapped.

· The Last Chapter ·
PUDDLEBY ONCE MORE

Never have I felt so utterly helpless in my life. While he spoke with the moth the giant held me down with his huge hand upon the insect's back. A cry, I thought, might still be worth attempting. I opened my mouth and bawled as hard as I could. Instantly the Moon Man's thumb came around and covered my face. He ceased speaking.

Soon I could feel from the stirring of the insect's legs that he was getting ready to fly. The Doctor could not reach me now in time, even if he had heard my cry. The giant removed his hand and left me free as the moth broke into a run. On either side of me the great wings spread out, acres-wide, to breast the air. In one last mad effort I raced over the left wing and took a flying leap. I landed at the giant's waistline and clung for all I was worth, still yelling lustily for the Doctor. The Moon Man picked me off and set me back upon the moth. But as my hold at his waist was wrenched loose, something ripped and came away in my hand. It was the masterpiece, the horn picture of Pippiteepa. In his anxiety to put me aboard Jamaro again, who was now racing over the ground at a terrible speed, he never noticed that I carried his treasure with me.

Nor indeed was I vastly concerned with it at the moment. My mind only contained one thought: I was being taken away from the Doctor. Apparently I was to be carried off alone and set back upon the earth. As the moth's speed increased still further I heard a fluttering near my right ear. I turned my head. And there, thank goodness, was Polynesia flying along like a swallow! In a torrent of words she poured out her message. For once in her life she was too pressed for time to swear.

"Tommy! They know the Doctor is worried about your staying away from your parents. I told him to be careful last night. They heard. They're afraid if you stay he'll want to leave too, to get you back. And—"

The moth's feet had left the ground and his nose was tilted upward to clear the tops of the trees that bordered the open space. The powerful rush of air, so familiar to me from my first voyage of this kind, was already beginning—and growing all the time. Flapping and beating, Polynesia put on her best speed and for a while longer managed to stay level with my giant airship.

"Don't worry, Tommy," she screeched. "I had an inkling of what the Moon Man had up his sleeve, though I couldn't find out where he was hiding. And I warned the Doctor. He gave me this last message for you, in case they should try to ship you out: Look

after the old lame horse in the stable. Give an eye to
the fruit trees. *And don't worry!* He'll find a way
down, all right, he says. Watch out for the second
smoke signal." (Polynesia's voice was growing faint,
and she was already dropping behind.) . . . "Good-
bye and good luck!"

I tried to shout an answer, but the rushing air
stopped my breath and made me gasp. "Good-bye
and good luck!" It was the last I heard from the
moon.

I lowered myself down among the deep fur to
avoid the pressure of the tearing wind. My groping
hands touched something strange. It was the moon
bells. The giant in sending me down to the earth had
thought of the needs of the human. I grabbed one of
the big flowers and held it handy to plunge my face
in. Bad times were coming, I knew when we must
cross the dead belt. There was nothing more I could
do for the present. I would lie still and take it easy till
I reached Puddleby and the little house with the big
garden.

Well, for the most part, my journey back was not
very different from our first voyage. If it was lonelier
for me than had been the trip with the Doctor, I, at all
events, had the comfort this time of knowing from
experience that the journey *could* be performed by a
human with safety.

But, dear me, what a sad trip it was! In addition to
my loneliness I had a terrible feeling of guilt. I was
leaving the Doctor behind—the Doctor who had
never abandoned me nor any friend in need. True, it
was not my fault, as I assured myself over and over

again. Yet I couldn't quite get rid of the idea that if I had only been a little more resourceful or quicker-witted, this would not have happened. And how, *how* was I going to face Dab-Dab, Jip, and the rest of them with the news that John Dolittle had been left in the moon?

The journey seemed endlessly long. Some fruit also had been provided, I found, by the Moon Man; but as soon as we approached the dead belt I felt too seasick to eat and remained so for the rest of the voyage.

At last, the motion abated enough to let me sit up and take observations. We were quite close to the earth. I could see it shining cheerfully in the sun, and the sight of it warmed my heart. I had not realized till then how homesick I had been for weeks past.

The moth landed me on Salisbury Plain. While not familiar with the district, I knew the spire of Salisbury Cathedral from pictures. And the sight of it across this flat characteristic country told me where I was. Apparently it was very early morning, though I had no idea of the exact hour.

The heavier air and gravity of the earth took a good deal of getting used to, after the very different conditions of the moon. Feeling like nothing so much as a ton weight of misery, I clambered down from the moth's back and took stock of my surroundings.

Morning mists were rolling and breaking over this flat piece of my native earth. From higher up it had seemed so sunny and homelike and friendly. Down here on closer acquaintance it didn't seem attractive at all.

Presently when the mists broke a little, I saw, not

far off, a road. A man was walking along it. A farm laborer, no doubt, going to his work. How small he seemed! Perhaps he was a dwarf. With a sudden longing for human company, I decided to speak to him. I lunged heavily forward (the trial of the disturbing journey and the unfamiliar balance of earth gravity together made me reel like a drunken man), and when I had come within twenty paces I hailed him. The results were astonishing, to say the least. He turned at the sound of my voice. His face went white as a sheet. Then he bolted like a rabbit and was gone into the mist.

I stood in the road down which he had disappeared. And suddenly it came over me what I was and how I must have looked. I had not measured myself recently on the moon but I did so soon after my return to the earth. My height was nine feet nine inches and my waist measurement fifty-one inches and a half. I was dressed in a homemade suit of bark and leaves. My shoes and leggings were made of root fiber and my hair was long enough to touch my shoulders.

No wonder the poor farmhand suddenly confronted by such an apparition on the wilds of Salisbury Plain had bolted! Suddenly I thought of Jamaro Bumblelily again. I would try to give him a message for the Doctor. If the moth could not understand me, I'd write something for him to carry back. I set out in search. But I never saw him again. Whether the mists misled me in direction or whether he had already departed moonward again I never found out.

So, here I was, a giant dressed like a scarecrow, no money in my pockets—no earthly possessions beyond a piece of reindeer horn, with a prehistoric picture carved on it. And then I realized, of course, that the farm laborer's reception of me would be what I would meet with everywhere. It was a long way from Salisbury to Puddleby, that I knew. I must have coachfare; I must have food.

I tramped along the road a while, thinking. I came in sight of a farmhouse. The appetizing smell of frying bacon reached me. I was terribly hungry. It was worth trying. I strode up to the door and knocked gently. A woman opened it. She gave one scream at sight of me and slammed the door in my face. A moment later a man threw open a window and leveled a shotgun at me.

"Get off the place," he snarled. "Quick! Or I'll blow your ugly head off."

More miserable than ever, I wandered on down the road. What was to become of me? There was no one to whom I could tell the truth. For who would believe my story? But I must get to Puddleby. I admitted I was not particularly keen to do that—to face the Dolittle household with the news. And yet I must. Even without the Doctor's last message about the old horse and the fruit trees, and the rest, it was my job— to do my best to take his place while he was away. And then my parents—poor folk! I fear I had forgotten them in my misery. And would even they recognize me now?

Then of a sudden I came upon a caravan of

Gypsies. They were camped in a thicket of gorse by the side of the road, and I had not seen them as I approached.

They, too, were cooking breakfast and more savory smells tantalized my empty stomach. It is rather strange that the Gypsies were the only people I met who were not afraid of me. They all came out of the wagons and gathered about me, gaping; but they were interested, not scared. Soon I was invited to sit down and eat. The head of the party, an old man, told me they were going on to a county fair and would be glad to have me come with them.

I agreed, with thanks. Any sort of friendship that would save me from an outcast's lot was something to be jumped at. I found out later that the old Gypsy's idea was to hire me off (at a commission) to a circus as a giant.

But, as a matter of fact, that lot, also, I was glad to accept when the time came. I had to have money. I could not appear in Puddleby like a scarecrow. I needed clothes, I needed coachfare, and I needed food to live on.

The circus proprietor—when I was introduced by my friend the Gypsy—turned out to be quite a decent fellow. He wanted to book me up for a year's engagement. But I of course refused. He suggested six months. Still I shook my head. My own idea was the shortest possible length of time that would earn me enough money to get back to Puddleby, looking decent. I guessed from the circus man's eagerness that he wanted me in his show at almost any cost and for almost any length of time. Finally, after much argument, we agreed upon a month.

Then came the question of clothes. At this point I was very cautious. He at first wanted me to keep my hair long and wear little more than a loin cloth. I was to be a "Missing Link from Mars," or something of the sort. I told him I didn't want to be anything of the kind (though his notion was much nearer to the truth than he knew). His next idea for me was the "Giant Cowboy from the Pampas." For this I was to wear an enormous sunhat, woolly trousers, pistols galore, and spurs with rowels like saucers. That didn't appeal to me either very much as a Sunday suit to show to Puddleby.

Finally, as I realized more fully how keen the showman was to have me, I thought I would try to arrange my own terms.

"Look here, sir," I said, "I have no desire to appear something I am not. I am a scientist, an explorer, returned from foreign parts. My great growth is a result of the climates I have been through and the diet I have had to live on. I will not deceive the public by masquerading as a Missing Link or Western Cowboy. Give me a decent suit of black, such as a man of learning would wear. And I will guarantee to tell your audiences tales of travel—true tales—such as they have never imagined in their wildest dreams. But I will not sign on for more than a month. That is my last word. Is it a bargain?"

Well, it was. He finally agreed to all my terms. My wages were to be three shillings a day. My clothes were to be my own property when I had concluded my engagement. I was to have a bed and a wagon to myself. My hours for public appearance were strictly laid down, and the rest of my time was to be my own.

It was not hard work. I went on show from ten to twelve in the morning, from three to five in the afternoon, and from eight to ten at night. A tailor was produced who fitted my enormous frame with a decent-looking suit. A barber was summoned to cut my hair. During my show hours I signed my autograph to pictures of myself that the circus proprietor had printed in great numbers. They were sold at threepence apiece. Twice a day I told the gaping crowds of holiday folk the story of my travels. But I never spoke of the moon. I called it just a "foreign land"— which, indeed, was true enough.

At last, the day of my release came. My contract was ended, and with three pounds, fifteen shillings in my pocket, and a good suit of clothes upon my back I was free to go where I wished. I took the first coach in the direction of Puddleby. Of course, many changes had to be made, and I was compelled to stop the night at one point before I could make connections for my native town.

On the way, because of my great size, I was stared and gaped at by all who saw me. But I did not mind it so much now. I knew that at least I was not a terrifying sight.

On reaching Puddleby at last, I decided I would call on my parents first, before I went to the Doctor's house. This may have been just a putting off of the evil hour. But, anyway, I had the good excuse that I should put an end to my parents' anxiety.

I found them just the same as they had always been —very glad to see me, eager for news of where I had gone and what I had done. I was astonished, however, that they had taken my unannounced departure so calmly—that is, I *was* astonished until it came out that having heard that the Doctor also had mysteriously disappeared, they had not been nearly so worried as they might have been. Such was their faith in the great man, like the confidence that all placed in him. If *he* had gone and taken me with him, then everything was surely all right.

I was glad, too, that they recognized me despite my unnatural size. Indeed I think they took a sort of pride in that I had, like Caesar, "grown so great." We sat in front of the fire, and I told them all of our adventures as well as I could remember them.

It seemed strange that they, simple people though they were, accepted my preposterous story of a journey to the moon with no vestige of doubt or disbelief. I feared there were no other humans in the world— outside of Matthew Mugg, who would so receive my statement. They asked me when I expected the Doctor's return. I told them what Polynesia had said of the second smoke signal, by which John Dolittle planned to notify me of his departure from the moon. But I had to admit I felt none too sure of his escape from a land where his services were so urgently demanded. Then when I almost broke down, accusing myself of abandoning the Doctor, they both comforted me with assurances that I could not have done more than I had.

Finally my mother insisted that I stay the night at their house and not attempt to notify the Dolittle household until the morrow. I was clearly overtired and worn out, she said. So, still willing to put off the evil hour, I persuaded myself that I *was* tired and turned in.

The next day I sought out Matthew Mugg, the cat's-meat man. I merely wanted his support when I should present myself at "the little house with the big garden." But it took me two hours to answer all the questions he fired at me about the moon and our voyage.

At last, I did get to the Doctor's house. My hand had hardly touched the gate latch before I was surrounded by them all. Too-Too, the vigilant sentinel, had probably been on duty ever since we left, and one hoot from him brought the whole family into the front garden like a fire alarm. A thousand exclamations and remarks about my increased growth and changed appearance filled the air. But there never was a doubt in their minds as to who I was.

And then suddenly a strange silence fell over them all when they saw that I had returned alone. Surrounded by them I entered the house and went to the kitchen. And there by the fireside, where the great man himself has so often sat and told us tales, I related the whole story of our visit to the moon.

At the end they were nearly all in tears, Gub-Gub howling out loud.

" 'Don't worry, Tommy, he'll come back' "

"We'll never see him again!" he wailed. "They'll never let him go. Oh, Tommy, how *could* you have left him?"

"Oh, be quiet!" snapped Jip. "He couldn't help it. He was kidnapped. Didn't he tell you? Don't worry. We'll watch for the smoke signal. John Dolittle will come back to us, never fear. Remember he has Polynesia with him."

"Aye!" squeaked the white mouse. "She'll find a way."

"*I* am not worried," sniffed Dab-Dab, brushing away her tears with one wing, and swatting some flies off the breadboard with the other. "But it's sort of lonely here without him."

"Tut-tut!" grunted Too-Too. "Of course he'll come back!"

There was a tapping at the window.

"Cheapside," said Dab-Dab. "Let him in, Tommy."

I lifted the sash and the cockney sparrow fluttered in and took his place upon the kitchen table, where he fell to picking up what bread crumbs had been left after the housekeeper's careful "clearing away." Too-Too told him the situation in a couple of sentences.

"Why, bless my heart!" said the sparrow. "Why all these long faces? John Dolittle stuck in the moon! Preposterous notion! *Pre*-posterous, I tell you! You couldn't get that man stuck nowhere. My word, Dab-Dab! When you clear away you don't leave much fodder behind, do you? Any mice what live in your 'ouse shouldn't 'ave no difficulty keepin' their figures."

Well, it was done. And I was glad to be back in the old house. I knew it was only a question of time before I would regain a normal size on a normal diet. Meanwhile, here I would not have to see anyone I did not want to.

And so I settled down to pruning the fruit trees, caring for the comfort of the old horse in the stable, and generally trying to take the Doctor's place as best I could. And night after night as the year wore on, Jip, Too-Too, and I would sit out, two at a time, while the moon was visible, to watch for the smoke signal. Often when we returned to the house with the daylight, discouraged and unhappy, Jip would rub his head against my leg and say:

"Don't worry, Tommy. He'll come back. Remember he has Polynesia with him. Between them they will find a way."

THE END

· About the Author ·

HUGH LOFTING was born in Maidenhead, England, in 1886 and was educated at home with his brothers and sister until he was eight. He studied engineering in London and at the Massachusetts Institute of Technology. After his marriage in 1912 he settled in the United States.

During World War One he left his job as a civil engineer, was commissioned a lieutenant in the Irish Guards, and found that writing illustrated letters to his children eased the strain of war. "There seemed to be very little to write to youngsters from the front; the news was either too horrible or too dull. One thing that kept forcing itself more and more upon my attention was the very considerable part the animals were playing in the war. That was the beginning of an idea: an eccentric country physician with a bent for natural history and a great love of pets. . . ."

These letters became *The Story of Doctor Dolittle*, published in 1920. Children all over the world have read this book and the eleven that followed, for they have been translated into almost every language. *The Voyages of Doctor Dolittle* won the Newbery Medal in 1923. Drawing from the twelve *Doctor Dolittle* volumes, Hugh Lofting's sister-in-law, Olga Fricker, later compiled *Doctor Dolittle: A Treasury,* which was published by Dell in 1986 as a Yearling Classic.

Hugh Lofting died in 1947 at his home in Topanga, California.